COLD CASE CONNECTION

DANA MENTINK

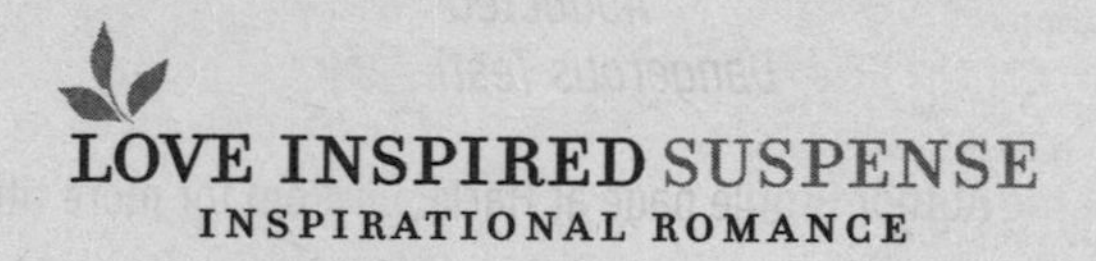

LOVE INSPIRED® SUSPENSE
INSPIRATIONAL ROMANCE

ISBN-13: 978-1-335-40263-9

Cold Case Connection

This edition published by arrangement with Harlequin Books S.A.

For questions and comments about the quality of this book, please contact us at CustomerService@Harlequin.com.

Love Inspired
22 Adelaide St. West, 40th Floor
Toronto, Ontario M5H 4E3, Canada
www.Harlequin.com

Printed in U.S.A.

Their car began to accelerate down the mountain.

"Slow down, Sergio," Helen cried.

"I can't. We have no brakes."

Inch by inch the SUV picked up speed. The black rocks of the cliffside streaked by as the car shimmied closer and closer to the edge of control.

Sergio downshifted, but the vehicle accelerated anyhow. As the rocks flashed by on either side of the car, he fought to keep to his side of the road. Their speed increased. He pumped the brakes frantically with no response.

"Jump out, Helen, before we're moving any faster."

"No."

"Listen..."

"Stop it, Sergio." Her words snapped out like the crackle of electricity. "I'm not leaving you, not like I did to your sister."

Sergio groaned. He'd thought everything between them was about Fiona, but now all he could hold on to was getting Helen safely out. In that moment everything vanished but the need to keep Helen safe...

Dana Mentink is a national bestselling author. She has been honored to win two Carol Awards, a HOLT Medallion and an RT Reviewers' Choice Best Book Award. She's authored more than thirty novels to date for Love Inspired Suspense and Harlequin Heartwarming. Dana loves feedback from her readers. Contact her at danamentink.com.

Books by Dana Mentink

Love Inspired Suspense

Roughwater Ranch Cowboys

Danger on the Ranch
Deadly Christmas Pretense
Cold Case Connection

Gold Country Cowboys

Cowboy Christmas Guardian
Treacherous Trails
Cowboy Bodyguard
Lost Christmas Memories

Pacific Coast Private Eyes

Dangerous Tidings
Seaside Secrets
Abducted
Dangerous Testimony

Visit the Author Profile page at Harlequin.com for more titles.

Dearly beloved, avenge not yourselves, but rather give place unto wrath: for it is written, Vengeance is mine; I will repay, saith the Lord.

—*Romans* 12:19

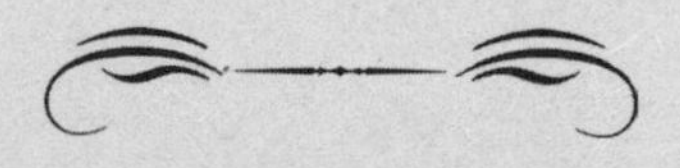

To all the single parents who are heroes to so many.

ONE

Helen Pike awoke with a jolt, cold sweat dappling her brow. For a shuddering moment, she thought she was back in the tunnels, a naive teen, on that terrible night that would not leave her soul. Cold stone, silence and an endless dripping echoed from the past. She rubbed her temples to massage the memories away.

That was fifteen years ago. You were a kid in high school. Are you ever going to let go of that nightmare?

For some inexplicable reason, she'd recently begun to relive the tragic event in her dreams. Five high school friends, Helen, Fiona, Trish, Gavin and Justin, had gone into the abandoned tunnels not more than two miles from the cottage where she now sat, but only four made it out alive. Trish had been murdered, her life ended on the frigid rock floor, her killer never caught.

Helen propped herself up on the musty couch and brushed her hair out of her face. The cottage, nestled on Roughwater Ranch property, was weakened by age and weather. Her stand-in parents Gus and Ginny Knightly, the ranch owners, had finally decided to have it demolished. That was fine by Helen, since it reminded her of yet another tragedy, one that she might have prevented, which hurt all the worse.

What happened with Trish was ancient history; losing one of her friends to murder should have been a once-in-a-lifetime thing. Yet three years ago, her other high school friend, Fiona Ross, had stayed in Driftwood, in this very cottage as a matter of fact, and she too had been murdered during that visit.

"An apparent hit-and-run," the police officer had said. "The driver didn't stop."

Didn't stop, and neither had the anguish that spawned in Helen that day. Two friends, two killings. She'd never thought the deaths could be related, but then she'd found the note four days ago, written in Fiona's hand, stuffed under the desk blotter.

Trish. Proof.

Find out who still has theirs.

Trish? The name was the tip of a nail, poking in her heart. *Proof?* The hammer plunging it deep.

What had Fiona been looking into? Why bring up the high school murder? Those long three years since Fiona was killed felt so fresh, Helen could recall the smell of the pink funeral carnations, hear the cries of Fiona's babies, the thin wails that reverberated over the gravestones and arrowed right to Helen's core. The girls were toddlers now, almost three. How would they remember their mother who'd missed out on so much?

Her phone buzzed with a reminder alarm, rattling her back to the present.

Ten at night. She needed to double-check the dining hall setup while the Roughwater Lodge was quiet, the guests all gone to bed for the night. No more time to putter about in this relic, looking for answers she'd never find. Maybe demolishing it would blast away her guilt too.

Something snapped outside, and she jerked to her feet, nerves taut. Most likely a deer? A coyote? Why had she come here so late at night?

Don't be a ninny—you're perfectly safe. The cottage was a short distance from the lodge which she managed for Gus and Ginny. They were like family to Helen, and she'd always affectionately called them aunt and uncle. The ranch was her home, workplace of her overprotective brother Liam, her adopted brothers Mitch Whitehorse and Chad Jaggert. Nothing could happen to her on this property.

But Fiona Ross was dead, just like Trish, and now she couldn't ignore the notion that the two were connected. Helen's conscience began its familiar badgering.

Why didn't you ask Fiona where she was going that day? Why she was distracted? Worried?

It was the list of questions Fiona's brother Sergio had flung at her the day of Fiona's funeral. Since then, he'd rebuffed every effort she'd made to reach out to the children, to try and connect in some small way with the little girls who'd lost their mother on her watch. Her cards were returned, her phone calls unanswered. He blamed her, but not as much as she blamed herself.

Helen tiptoed to the window and looked out into a thick screen of oak and pine. The branches dripped with moisture from the brewing January storm that swept in from the ocean across the acres of ranch property. She could make out nothing sinister in the damp night, no monsters or bogeymen.

Maybe it was her imagination stoking her paranoia. Certainly that seemed to be the opinion of Mark Farraday, the police chief standing in for Danny Patron who had taken a leave of absence. Chief Farraday merely raised a skeptical eyebrow when she'd presented Fiona's note.

Helen had begun to doubt herself. Could it be mere coincidence that Fiona had scrawled that message just before she was killed?

Snap.

Now the sound came from the rear. She gulped in a breath. Surely not, more likely it was outside, some animal looking for shelter. Still, she gripped the phone in her pocket. Should she call the police? And tell them what? She'd heard a noise?

She shook her head. Any other time she would have texted her brother Liam, but he was away with his new bride Maggie on their honeymoon. Chad? The poor guy was probably exhausted after assisting the vet all day with inoculating the herd.

Big-girl time, Helen. Go get in your car and drive away.

She'd reached for the front doorknob when a crash of breaking glass and a sudden whoosh of air rushed through the house along with a bang that shook the walls. She screamed and yanked the door open and was halfway to her car when she realized what must have happened. The mangled edge of a tree limb protruded from the shattered glass. A branch from the aged oak had come loose and crashed through the side bedroom window. It took several steadying breaths before she could laugh at her own terror.

No fancy double-paned windows here, the cottage was outdated, damaged by an earthquake that had rumbled across the region some months prior.

Teeth gritted, Helen retraced her steps. No reason to leave glass strewn everywhere. The very idea of it aggravated her need for tidiness, which Liam said bordered on obsession. She tried to flick on the lights. Nothing. The power had gone out due to the howling storm. Instead she activated her phone light and grabbed the broom and dustpan from the hall closet, bumping it closed with her hip.

Cold winter air barreled through the fractured window, chilling her fingers, snaking up her spine. She cleaned up as best she could, dumping the broken glass in a trash bin under the kitchen sink.

Holding the dustpan and broom, she went to the closet to return the items.

Fright gripped her stomach. The closet door was a few inches ajar, the door she'd closed tight not a few moments before.

Her skin pimpled with goose bumps.

The wind, it had to be. But the wind would blow against the door and close it, not open it from the inside. She tried to reason with her trembling nerves.

It just came open, that's all. Old structure, unsettled foundation.

She blew out a breath. Did she used to be a nervous Nellie? Scared of her own shadow? With conviction, she reached out to pull it all the way open when it shot wide, the door cracking into her forehead, sending her to the floor.

Sergio chafed against the seat belt. He longed for his motorcycle, to feel the unfettered freedom of a V-twin engine and an endless stretch of open road. But motorcycles were wildly impractical for transporting a pair of almost-three-year-old girls. He still felt the stab of pain at selling his beloved bike. The used SUV that now took him down the country road was sensible, safe…completely boring. It was a humdrum ride, complete with two empty car seats at the moment, strapped snugly into the back since the girls were safely at the hotel with their nanny. At least his ride didn't have a stick-figure-family decal on the rear window. There really was no sticker that could adequately capture the misfit family he was so desperately trying to hold together anyway, Uncle Sergio and his sister's daughters. No, *his* daughters now.

Daddy. Their sole provider. Responsible for everything from trimming their toenails to encouraging their empathy. That last one was tricky, since he wasn't sure he had any himself. Not anymore.

When the tension seized his gut, he tried to reassure himself.

Laurel and Lucy were okay, weren't they? Mostly happy and healthy? So maybe he didn't always know exactly how to handle it when they cried or lost their favorite snuggle toys, but he'd weathered the storms as they came and tried to keep his sister's memory alive for them as best he could. He'd given up on telling them much about their father, the man who'd died of an aneurysm just before they were born. That had been tragic enough, but to lose their mother when they were only a few months old?

The relentless barrage of their needs sometimes made him long for his work, diving in bottomless oceans, alone, with nothing but the sound of his own breathing in his Scuba regulator. But getting his PI license meant he could be there for the girls, and their needs trumped his. "And don't you worry, girls," he muttered to himself. "Your mama's killer is going to pay."

A gust of wind sent leaves scuttling across his windshield and snapped him out of his reverie. He figured he might have strayed onto private property, but he had seen no sign and there hadn't been a fence barring the way. He wasn't there to make trouble, just to lay eyes on the place. In his rare imaginative moments, Sergio sometimes fancied himself a spider, so intricate was the web he'd spun, the feelers he'd put into place to solve the mystery of Fiona's murder.

Those feelers had begun to vibrate when he'd learned that Helen Pike had gone to the cops with a note she'd found from Fiona.

Trish. Proof.

Find out who still has theirs.

It meant nothing to him. Was Helen making something up in her mind? Imagining a connection between what happened to Trish all those years ago and his sister? Maybe Helen's own guilt had finally gotten the better of her. He felt no pity. She should have listened to Fiona, gone with her on whatever crazy investigation she'd hinted at in her last message to him.

Sorry I missed your call, Serg. Going to talk to Helen about something that's bothering me. She'll help me. Some help. Helen admitted to him that she'd put Fiona off, busy with her duties managing her fancy hotel. Helen's tear-washed jade eyes had not cooled his ire one bit. His sister was gone, his nieces left orphaned with only a hard-bitten, desperate uncle to care for them.

He had a fleeting thought that he hadn't reminded

Laurel and Lucy to brush their teeth. Yet another thing he'd have to hope the nanny followed through on.

You're a sad excuse for a parent, Serg.

A cottage came into view that had to be the one he sought. Parked outside was a van with Roughwater Lodge emblazoned on the side. As he opened the car door, his nose picked up the clue before his brain did.

Smoke.

A fire in the fireplace?

Yet the cottage was dark.

Not completely dark. There was a flicker of orange like a monarch flitting against the front window.

Not a monarch, his brain finally supplied.

A flame.

The cottage was burning. His leather boots hit the ground with a smack as he barreled out of the SUV and shoved through the front door.

"Hey," he yelled. "Anybody in here?"

No answer. The curtains in the shabby front room were on fire, a lighter still lit on the floor, one of those fancy numbers that kept burning until it was switched off. The flames had not yet started to devour the rest of the room. Smoke filtered through the air, mingling with the darkness, so he did not notice at first.

As he lurched toward the curtains to pull them down and stomp out the flames, his boot impacted something soft. No, not something…someone!

TWO

Helen's senses flooded her brain with disconnected impressions: heat, smoke, pain and the sensation of someone reaching for her, grabbing her arms. Her brother Liam? Returned early from his honeymoon to help her? No, someone else, a stranger, there in the shadows of the burning house. Her consciousness returned with a mighty rush of adrenaline. She sprang up and shoved the hands away.

"Don't touch me."

"Easy," said a voice through the smoke in a raspy baritone. "Just trying to help."

Helen shimmied backward until her shoulders hit the wall. The burning curtains backlit a towering man wearing a leather jacket and boots, mussed black hair that needed a trim. There was something familiar about him, the set of his square jaw, the wide brace of shoulders, five-o'clock shadow. Smoke tickled her throat and she coughed. "What…what happened?"

"That's my question. First thing's first. We'll talk outside."

When she didn't move, he took her arm and guided her toward the front door and out into the wind-tossed night. She stumbled on the grass made uneven by tunneling rodents, sinking to one knee. As he bent over to assist, she felt the ground vibrating. A horse and rider wheeled to a stop, sending bits of mud whirling into the air.

Chad slid off the horse, rifle at his shoulder, trained on the other man. “Get away from her or you’re dead.”

Her rescuer raised his palms. “Look, John Wayne, no need to shoot me. I’m a Good Samaritan. Cottage is burning. She needed help getting out.”

“You’re trespassing. This is private property.” Chad had not lowered the gun.

The man lifted a careless shoulder. “I missed the signs, or you need better ones.”

Helen realized her skull was pounding with pain. She fingered a bump on her forehead.

“You okay, Helen?” Chad said.

She heard the man next to her release a bitter sigh. “Helen,” he said softly. “Figures.”

“And you are?” Chad snapped.

“Sergio Ross.” There was a hard-edged challenge in his voice. “Maybe you knew my sister, Fiona. She was murdered here in your quaint little town. She stayed right in this cottage, as a matter of fact.”

Helen’s insides twisted. Sergio Ross. She flashed back to the funeral, Sergio’s face stark with pain, two little babies cradled in his arms as he bid goodbye to his sister, their mother, her best friend.

She gulped in a breath and fought for calm. “It’s all right, Chad,” she said. “I’m okay. He’s…he’s not here to hurt me.” But he did, just with his presence, the blame that emanated from him in silent waves.

Chad finally lowered the rifle, putting it aside to ease next to Helen.

Sergio strode back toward the burning cabin.

"Where are you going?" she called.

"To put out the fire. Not too big yet. I can rip down the curtains and smother it before it gets a real foothold."

"Place is slated for demolition," Chad said to his back, tone still hostile. "Not worth getting hurt over."

"It's no bother." Sergio climbed the porch step. "Police are gonna need to photograph and such."

Police. The word cinched something tight inside her.

"Police?" Chad looked from Sergio to Helen. "Someone set the fire?"

Helen tried and failed to put the confused pieces into place. "I'm not sure."

"I am," Sergio said. "The lighter on the floor was a dead giveaway." He paused. "Unless you've taken up cigarette smoking, Helen?"

His words were acid. She wrapped her arms around herself, trying to keep straight against his disdain. "No."

Sergio bobbed a chin. "Fine then. Maybe Cowboy Chad here can call the cops while I put out the fire." He vanished into the smoky interior.

Chad raised an eyebrow, his normally impassive face troubled as he pulled out his cell phone. "So that's Sergio Ross?"

She nodded.

"What's he doing here?"

It was the very same question making painful circles in her mind.

Sergio Ross.

The last man on earth she wanted to see.

Sergio wondered if the tension he was picking up was from the cop, the cowboy clan who were seemingly coming out of the woodwork or his own angst at returning to the town that had claimed his sister's life. Probably all of the above, he decided.

Property owners Gus and Ginny Knightly were cordial to him and comforting to Helen, inviting the cop and participants back to the warmth of their beautiful Spanish-style ranch house to finish the questioning. Helen sat across the room on an armchair, being fussed over by Ginny. He could see she was developing a decent-sized bruise on her forehead. She'd shared what facts she knew. The branch that came through the window was a ruse, he suspected, to urge her out of the cottage, probably an attempt to get her to leave. The person then circled around and hid in the closet, perhaps not expecting her to fetch the broom. When she awoke the place was on fire.

The cop waiting patiently for his statement looked to Sergio to be in his late sixties, face wide, head shaved, tanned from time out in the sun, pretty fit from the looks of him. "I'm Mark Farraday, acting chief of the Driftwood Police Department."

"Where's the real chief?" Sergio asked mildly, earning himself a sharp look which he deserved.

"Danny Patron is on leave," Farraday said. "His youngest just had a liver transplant."

Sergio's heart thudded considering what that must feel like, to watch your child struggle for their life. He jammed his hands in his pockets, regretting his gibe.

Farraday shoved a stick of gum into his mouth and chewed for a moment. "You're a commercial diver?"

The cop had done a little checking. "I was."

"What kind?"

"Deadhead logger." He caught the blank look. "I work for a company that salvages sinker logs."

Surprisingly it was Chad who spoke up. "Some of

those logs were cut way back in the 1800s. The water keeps them pristine. They're worth big money." Chad cocked his chin. "Risky job."

"Can be." He thought he detected a glimmer of respect in the younger man's eyes, which vanished in an instant.

Farraday continued. "So what brings you to the ranch? To Driftwood?"

"Up from southern California. Visiting."

He raised an eyebrow. "Not investigating?"

Sergio smiled. The cop was putting him on notice, establishing that he had the intel. "I am a licensed private investigator, as you already know, right? I came to the cottage because it's where my sister stayed before her death."

He saw Helen flinch. The bruise marred her skin, her dusting of freckles stark against the pale complexion. He saw the fine muscles of her throat convulse. It made him uncomfortable, though he couldn't figure out why. "Are you okay?" he asked before he could stop himself.

She pinched her lips together and nodded, meeting his gaze for a moment. The green of those eyes had to be one in a million, the iridescent hue of some brilliant ocean coral he'd photographed. He shook off the thought and went on. "I just wanted to see the place again before it was demolished."

"And?" Farraday prodded.

"And I got wind that there may be a connection between Fiona's death and the teen who was murdered, Trish O'Brian."

Now Farraday's eyes slitted. "How exactly did you get wind of that?"

Sergio shrugged. "Not important." Before Farraday could press him further he continued. "You were the investigating officer back at the time Trish was killed, weren't you?"

"Yes." One clipped syllable.

"And the murderer was never apprehended?"

Farraday paused. "No."

Sergio nodded. "The two kids who looked like suspects, Justin Dover and Gavin Cutter. Both were cleared." He shot a glance at Helen. "And you, and my sister, of course."

Farraday didn't respond.

"Now those tunnels where she died are closed up, but rumor has it they've been used more recently." Sergio surveyed the family watching his every move. "Bad guys get paid a few bucks to carry illegal prescription drugs from a drop to some distribution points."

"Old news. Patron shut that operation down. Those are rumors," Farraday said. "Plenty of those flying around in a small town. Don't believe everything you hear."

And don't discount anything either. "My sister was looking into something."

"Yes," Helen said, stepping around Ginny. He half expected Farraday to stop her joining them, but he didn't. She was followed by the cowboy he'd met earlier, Chad, and a mountain of a man with dusky skin and a scar on his cheek.

"Mitch Whitehorse," he said by way of introduction. "Helen's brother."

Not blood kin, clearly. The woman was surrounded by adopted cowboy brothers.

"Mitch is a former US marshal," Farraday explained. "He can tell you we don't arrest people without evidence, and there wasn't enough to nail anyone for Trish's death."

"Or my sister's."

Farraday nodded. "Correct."

"So the note? The one my sister wrote mentioning Trish before she was murdered?"

"Your sister's death was a hit-and-run..." the cop started.

"Murder," Sergio said firmly. "It's murder when a driver speeds up intentionally to hit someone and doesn't stop after, isn't that right?" He locked gazes with Helen again, noting something stark and anguished in her expression.

Farraday pushed back his chair and stood. "So why are you here, Mr. Ross? Are you intending to involve yourself in police business?"

"No." He felt every eye on him, suspicious, wary, waiting. "I'm here to make sure whoever killed my sister is sent to prison."

The room went dead silent.

Mitch spoke first, staring him down. "And who do you figure is responsible?"

Sergio wasn't about to be intimidated. "I don't know. I'll share when I have something concrete. Until then, I'll keep my investigation private."

Mitch's expression turned to granite. "Helen is our sister, and whoever was hiding in that closet hurt her and set fire to the cabin. We take that kind of thing real personally here at Roughwater Ranch, Mr. Ross."

"My sister was murdered here," he said, on his feet now. "And I take that personally too." He was almost as tall as Mitch and he leveraged every inch. Five tense seconds passed between them before he figured Mitch had got the measure of him. Helen stepped between them, her palm gentle on Mitch's wide chest.

"It's okay, Mitch," she whispered.

"No, it's not," Sergio said quietly. "It won't ever be all right because my sister is dead and her girls are motherless." He'd dropped the words like empty bottles that shattered on the tile floor. Shards of his anger struck at her and though he felt a flicker of shame, it did not blunt his rage. Her eyes raked him, searching. What was she looking for? Some of Fiona's warmth mirrored in him? She wasn't going to find it.

I'm all hard edges and determination, and I want only one thing.

Whoever killed Fiona is going to pay.

THREE

Helen refused a trip to the hospital. "It's a bump, that's all." And she declined to be persuaded to sleep at the ranch house. "I have to get back to the lodge. We've got a big group checking in in the morning, fifty cattlemen and women here for a convention."

She accepted hugs and kisses from a worried Gus and Ginny, and the promise that Farraday would process the cottage for evidence as soon as he finished with their statements. Chad walked her to her vehicle. She pretended not to notice Sergio trailing behind them, but his proximity made her senses prickle.

He'd become a private investigator, apparently, in the nearly three years since the funeral, and now he thought he was ready to solve his sister's murder.

Trish. Proof.

Find out who still has theirs.

Helen had noticed Fiona was distracted during her visit, but she assumed it was the responsibility of being a new mom. Helen had been knee-deep in responsibility herself at that time, having recently taken over the job as manager of the luxurious Roughwater Lodge. The town and lodge were bustling with people visiting the area for a horse show and competition. The morning of Fiona's death they were supposed to meet for coffee in town, but a broken water heater required Helen's attention and she'd postponed.

No prob, Fiona had messaged. Tell you about it later.

She hadn't even read the message until hours later, after Fiona had already been killed.

She realized they were at her van when Chad politely cleared his throat. Chad was a man of very few words, but she knew he wanted to be sure she was okay.

"Uh… I wondered if, you know, I should tell Liam," Chad said.

Her brother, the overprotective former Green Beret, would go bananas and Helen couldn't allow it. He and his new wife Maggie were in Tahiti, celebrating their marriage. Liam was happy for the first time in a very long while, in spite of the condition which was gradually stripping away his hearing. Ever since they were children, Liam had made Helen his number-one priority. It was time for him to do that for his new wife. She fixed Chad with her sternest look. "Don't you dare tell him."

Chad looked as though he'd swallowed something prickly. "Don't like secrets."

"I'll explain it all when he gets back. Promise."

Chad arched an eyebrow. "Gonna skin us both for keeping things from him."

She smiled and hugged the man who was as much her brother as if they had grown up together. "I can handle Liam."

"Not sure I can. He's gonna have me mucking stables until I'm eighty."

She laughed. "I promise, I will explain it all to him so he'll understand."

Chad's expression remained doubtful, but he opened the van door for her anyway.

"Mind if I have a word?"

Helen tensed to find Sergio standing a respectful distance behind, hands shoved in the pockets of his leather jacket.

Chad looked from him to her. He shot her a look that said, *Just say the word and I'll toss him off the property in a heartbeat.*

They were going to have to talk privately sooner or later. She forced a smile. "It's okay, Chad. It will just take a minute, and then I'll drive myself back to the lodge."

Reluctantly, he walked away a few paces toward the house, taking his time, keeping them in his peripheral vision. Her heart swelled at the family she'd found here at the ranch, a family she would do anything to protect.

Like you failed to do with Fiona?

She blinked the thoughts away and faced Sergio, searching for a way to make normal conversation. "How… I mean, where are you staying?"

"That's what I wanted to talk to you about."

"Oh?"

"Yeah. Got us a hotel suite, me and the girls and Miss Betty. That's their nanny."

The girls. Her breath caught. "They must be almost three now."

"Their birthday is coming up." His mouth worked for a moment. "Gotta…plan something, I guess. Preschool birthday parties aren't in my wheelhouse. Anyway, I need a better place. Hotel isn't comfortable for them and I'm sleeping on a rollaway which is about six inches too short. We need three rooms. I thought the lodge might suit, if you have vacancies."

The lodge? He wanted to stay at the lodge? "I…" *Stop stumbling around it.* She squared her shoulders. "I wouldn't think you'd want to stay there, at my place, frankly, since you blame me for Fiona's death."

His lips twitched. "I know you loved my sister and I know you didn't want harm to come to her, but yes, I blame you for letting her down."

Helen felt it like a slap, and the pain settled down into the reservoir of guilt she always carried around. "If it makes you feel better, I blame myself too, every day," she said quietly.

Silence swelled between them like a billowing cloud of smoke.

Sergio looked up toward the concealed moon and exhaled long and slow.

"How did you know I went to the police?" she asked.

He shrugged. "Not important. But in my mind, it's plenty to reopen an investigation. Could be you rattled someone's cage and they're nervous, looking for something Fiona might have left behind. Maybe they decided to destroy the cottage rather than risk you finding something else."

"Chief Farraday didn't see it that way."

"I get that sense. I'm going to stay until I bust the guy who killed Fiona, providing I can find a comfortable place for my girls."

My girls.

He continued. "We have a home in San Diego, nice enough, and Betty's incredible, but I don't want to be away from them for too long. Laurel is pretty self-confident, but Lucy gets anxious when I'm away. She won't eat properly and she cries."

Helen struggled for control at the reminder. Lucy. Fiona had given her daughter Helen's middle name. "I have a cabin," she said promptly. "It's away from the main house, not as many amenities, but it has three bedrooms, two bathrooms and a little kitchen. I was keeping it vacant for the painters to come in. You can stay there, you and the girls and Betty."

"Thank you," he said. "I'll pay whatever you ask."

"No need..."

"Yes, there is. We pay our own way," Sergio said quickly. She didn't miss the bitterness. "We're not taking anything from you."

Not taking anything from the woman who let his sister die.

I blame you for letting her down.

All right. If that's what needed to happen to help Fiona's little girls, she'd have to find a way to live with Sergio staying on the property. Exhaustion throbbed through her along with the pain in her forehead.

Lord, help me do what's right here.

She wished it did not involve Sergio Ross.

Sergio prepared the cabin as best he could for the girls. It was too late in the evening to move them. Betty told him over the phone that she'd finally gotten them to sleep and unless he wanted to see an epic temper tantrum thrown by a sixty-five-year-old woman, he would not be disturbing them this evening. As always, he deferred to her. Betty was a tell-it-like-it is, gray-haired, jewelry-obsessed, Sudoku-playing gift from God. He would have collapsed under the weight of his own parenting failures without her.

The cabin was small, and it warmed nicely when he flicked on the heater. Helen had sent over a housekeeper to put clean linens on the beds, and she refreshed the kitchen supply of coffee and snacks, including the fishy crackers the girls never got tired of. How had she known to include those? It wasn't until the housekeeper left that he saw the two coloring books with chunky crayons on the coffee table. A thoughtful gesture.

Helen had always been thoughtful, quiet, he remembered from the times she'd visited their cramped house in Driftwood during his senior year. He had to admit she'd grown into a beauty. There was something classy about Helen that made her a perfect fit to run a luxury lodge, right down to the barest hint of a lush Southern drawl in her voice. Antsy, he strolled to the window.

Their cabin was set out on a wide grassy area, shrouded with dripping oak trees and near a small fenced paddock where several horses stood silent sentry under the lean-to. They were there, no doubt, for guests to explore the riding trails that crisscrossed the wooded property. Sergio had spent many summers working as a wilderness guide and he missed those days in the saddle. He had a sudden warmth in his chest when he considered that maybe he could teach the girls to ride.

Would Fiona have wanted that? It was the question that constantly paralyzed him. She was ultracautious with their safety when they were infants, at least in the few times he'd visited after their birth. Even though they weren't crawling, she'd stopped up the outlets with plug protectors and dug up all the plants in the yard that might be poisonous. She'd treated them like fragile eggs that could be damaged at any time. But surely she would have wanted them to have experiences as they grew. Not to be cloistered, Bubble Wrapped against life. He frowned. Or was he trying to persuade himself because of his own thrill-seeking bent? He was a wanderer. He felt a hot flash of guilt. The girls had transformed his heart and he would die for them, but sometimes he could not help but miss his old life.

Restless, he went to the kitchen for a bottle of water. It was late, after midnight, but his thoughts refused to be wrangled. He spotted a Bible on the table and his gut twisted further. One thing he knew for certain was that Fiona wanted her daughters to love God and trust Him as their ultimate security. And how was he supposed to teach them that when God had saddled them with an uncle who had to watch YouTube videos even to figure out how to braid their hair?

On the prickly heels of those musings, he flopped down on the sofa and flung an arm over his eyes. One day at a time, he told himself. He held on to one phrase his mother told him on a regular basis. *Remember that God loves the girls more than you ever could.* God sure had a funny way of showing it.

He awakened some hours later. His cell told him it was four thirty, still well before sunup. It took him a moment to recall where he was until he heard a soft whinny. He sat up, blinking, and pulled aside the curtain. The storm had passed, and the moonlight lent enough glow for him to see someone out in the paddock saddling a horse. Even in the dim light he recognized Helen's slim figure, though her hair was down instead of twisted into its normal chignon, and she wore jeans and a warm jacket.

He rechecked the time to see if he'd been mistaken.

Not even sunup and she was heading out on a ride? That seemed odd, especially when she'd spoken about a large group checking in. Letting himself out of the cabin he approached quietly, coming close enough that he could hear her murmuring sweetly to the horse.

"Early morning ride?"

She jumped and squealed, one hand on the reins, the other over her heart. "You scared me."

"Sorry. Just wondered where you were going so early."

She cocked her head, the moonlight bathing her skin in pearl. "Just out for some air."

"Where?"

She didn't answer for a moment. "Is that your business?"

"Nope, but I'm wondering anyway. Fiona always said I was nosy."

A flicker of a smile crossed her lips. "I wanted to see something, is all."

"What?"

"Your sister was right, you are nosy." She huffed out a breath which misted in the cold. "The tunnels. Fiona asked me what I remembered about…about the night Trish died. We'd planned to ride out there, were going to talk about it at coffee but…" She broke off.

"You didn't because she was killed."

Helen's mouth trembled, or perhaps it was the trick of the moonlight. He shifted. "So you're going to ride out there to see if anything comes back to you?"

"Basically, yes."

"All by yourself?"

"I have to be back here in a few hours. It's now or never."

"I'll go with you." He strode toward the tack shed and helped himself to a saddle, outfitting the big gelding that he figured could handle his six foot two easily enough.

"I don't..."

"Want me to go?" He climbed into the saddle. "Going to follow you one way or the other so we might as well get at it."

"This is a waste of time. There's nothing there in those tunnels after all these years."

"If my sister was interested, it's not a waste of time. Let's go. You've got a group of cattlemen to check in, remember?"

Helen climbed easily into the saddle, though she looked anything but calm. They set off at a brisk pace, and he followed her lead. She obviously knew the area well and she was an excellent horsewoman, adjusting smoothly to the mare's movements. The trail bisected the lodge property until it pitched sharply upward, the ground becoming rocky and thick with oak and eucalyptus. In spite of the circumstances, he found himself enjoying the ride, the joy of being outside, moving freely, and, though he didn't want to admit it, a break from the constant worry over a certain pair of adorable twin girls. The farther they progressed under the dripping trees, the more the tense coil inside him began to relax.

When they emerged at a granite outcropping, he glimpsed the sea in the distance, waves glimmering pewter in the predawn hours. He soaked in the wide expanse of God-breathed beauty.

"There," she said, interrupting his thoughts, pointing to a hillock he hadn't even noticed. It was peppered with hunks of granite but when he looked closer he could detect the outline of an opening, bordered in rotting wood. A sign that said Danger, Keep Out was wired to a sturdy metal grate.

"The perfect high school hangout," Sergio said. He wished he hadn't, when he caught the stark emotion on her face. This wasn't a place she wanted to come; it was a place where her childhood innocence had died along with her friend. "Uh, sorry. Bad joke." *Really bad.*

She didn't reply as they tied the horses to a limb and crossed the wet grass. Still silent, he thought she wouldn't speak at all until she shivered, her words sounding hollow, as if she'd been sucked back into that long-ago day.

"It was all supposed to be such fun. The abandoned tunnels were the coolest place to explore. They were originally used to haul ore from the mines down to the docks and onto the waiting ships. We'd looked around a bit before, but that night, we were going to have a competition, to see who could find their way out and meet up again by midnight." Her voice dropped to a whisper. "It was just a silly game."

"You and Fiona, Gavin and Justin, and Trish."

Helen nodded. "It was going to be a fun night. Trish had gone out on a few dates with Gavin, and we thought he was going to ask her to prom in the tunnels. Trish told us she'd seen a brochure for a tuxedo place in his backpack."

"And Justin? Did he have a girlfriend? Fiona? You maybe?"

She blushed and shook her head. "We were just friends. Justin was always the cutup, the funny guy. He liked Trish, too, but he didn't pursue her."

"That you know of."

"Yes." Her mind was far away, back in those tunnels. She was shivering in earnest now, and he'd started to shrug off his jacket to drape it over her when a motor rumbled through the night. They whirled to see a light bearing down on them from the hilltop, a man on some sort of vehicle.

"Sergio…" Helen started. She'd not gotten the next word out before a spray of bullets erupted around them.

FOUR

Helen could not process what was happening. Her ears throbbed from the sound of the shots and she was all over goose bumps. Sergio grabbed her hand and pulled her down behind a screen of bushes.

"Stay low as you can get," he whispered.

"Did someone just shoot at us?"

Sergio wasn't listening, instead peering through the branches. "The guy on an ATV that just rolled up." He took out his cell phone and growled. "No service." He took a picture of the approaching man.

Helen saw through the branches that the man, short, with a mop of curly hair, was getting off his vehicle, gun held ready, walking warily toward the place where she and Sergio crouched.

He murmured in her ear. "I'm going to buy some time. Get away from here. Too risky to go for the horses so run back toward the road if you can."

"Sergio…" she started, but he stood up and strode out of the bushes.

Run to the road like he told her? But she could not leave him to be killed. Her imagination ran wild for a moment, picturing another funeral, another loss for Fiona's twin girls. She could not, would not, be responsible for causing the children another moment of pain. She stood instead, creeping out after him.

Sergio was standing with his palms up, facing the man who now held a rifle trained on him. When she drew nearer, Sergio shot her a look of pure anger, a vein in his jaw pulsing.

She didn't look at him, beaming all her outrage on the guy in front of her. "What do you think you're doing firing on us? This is public land."

The shooter stared at her. "Tunnels are dangerous. I help the police keep an eye out for kids."

"Farraday?" Sergio's mouth pinched. "So you're telling me the police chief gives you permission to shoot at people?"

He shrugged. "Ah, don't be melodramatic. I wasn't anywhere near hitting you."

"Near enough," Sergio spat.

The man shrugged.

"Your name?" Sergio said.

"Kyle."

"Kyle what?" Sergio's tone was flint hard. When he didn't reply, Sergio's cheeks went dusky. "You could have killed us."

A cruel smile came and went on the guy's face. "If I'd wanted to kill you, you'd be dead."

"So your intention was to scare us?"

Kyle shrugged. "Like I said, kids can get hurt in the tunnels."

"Do we look like kids to you?"

Kyle tapped a finger to his brow and shrugged. "Nearsighted."

"Then get yourself some glasses before you murder someone," Sergio snapped.

Helen got a fleeting impression that murder might be something the gunman was familiar with already. "Since this is public property, we're fully within our rights to be here."

Kyle shrugged. "Me too, but if you're going to go butting into those tunnels like a couple of wandering fools, I'm going to stay on you until you leave, to tell the police where to find your bodies." He laughed. "You won't be the first girl found dead in those tunnels, right?"

Sergio jerked forward, but Helen swallowed her flush of panic. "I'm calling the police," Helen said. "And you can explain it all to Chief Farraday."

Kyle offered a careless nod. "You gotta hike to the peak to get a signal but go ahead. Farraday will understand. Simple mistake."

Farraday will understand. Something in those words struck a note of alarm deep in her stomach. Almost like he knew how Farraday would react.

Sergio took her wrist. "We're going. We'll saddle up and ride out of here. I already texted your photo to a friend so if we don't show up in perfect health back at the lodge, the photo will go to the cops and all over my friend's social media sites. Farraday isn't gonna like that, I'm guessing. You got me?"

Kyle didn't acknowledge. He still cradled his gun as Sergio led Helen away. The sound of a round being racked into the chamber made her jerk, but Sergio continued to lead her. The hairs on the back of her neck prickled as she imagined a bullet plowing through her spine.

"And tell Farraday I want to talk to him," Sergio tossed over his shoulder.

"Sure. Be careful on your way home," Kyle called.

"Driftwood isn't the peaceful little town people think it is."

Sergio turned back and Helen forced herself to as well, though her nerves were shouting at her to sprint away.

"Is that a threat?" Sergio said.

Kyle did not answer, so they continued on and retrieved the horses.

"Don't stop until we're clear," Sergio said, bringing his horse into line behind hers.

It wasn't until they'd returned to the gentle path that led onto lodge property that he brought his horse to a stop, black eyes sparking with fury. "You should have left like I told you."

She stared right back. "You needed backup."

"I didn't need anything of the kind, and you shouldn't have risked your safety."

"I let Fiona down. I'm not going to make that same mistake with her brother."

He blinked, looked away for a moment, muttering something, before he snapped his gaze back to her. "Let's get something straight right now. I don't want you or need you involved in this investigation. Am I clear?"

"Like crystal," she said. "But you're on my family property, riding my horse, and you're here because I went to the police, so I'm already involved in this investigation and I don't appreciate your tone."

His eyes narrowed. "I..." Then he huffed out a breath and tipped his head to the sky. "I apologize."

"Thank you."

"But I want to handle this case by myself."

"I understand, and I won't go out of my way to annoy

you, I promise." She raised an eyebrow. "Did you really text a picture of that guy?"

He grinned. "Yep, but it probably didn't go through anyway. Even so, I didn't have time to write a proper text to send with it, so if it did work, Miss Betty is probably wondering what in the world she's supposed to do with that photo."

Helen laughed. "Poor Miss Betty."

"No worries. The woman is made of tough stuff. She raised five boys."

Helen's limbs quivered, perhaps the delayed shock at what they'd just experienced.

His half smile faded, and he looked closely at her, causing warmth to climb into her cheeks. "You okay?"

"Yes. Why do you ask?"

"You look shaky. It's not every day you get fired at, and last night you got knocked down and your cabin set on fire."

"I'm all right, just trying to figure out what's going on here."

"Me too. I plan to find out exactly why Farraday doesn't want us in those tunnels and why he doesn't seem to be inclined to treat my sister's death as a murder."

"Maybe she left some other clue in the cabin. I'll..."

"No." He slid from the horse and offered her a hand for her to dismount. "Like I said, Helen, I don't need your help."

No, he wouldn't take any help from the woman who'd let his sister down. She flinched at the reminder; the flicker of bitterness in his expression told her that recent events aside, he had not changed his mind. She was to blame for Fiona's death. End of story. Avoiding his touch, she slid off the horse and led her back to the corral. Sergio did the same with the gelding.

She was trying to decide how best to gracefully take her leave when the door of the cabin flew open and a petite dark-haired girl darted out, followed by an older woman with another child walking close beside. The woman had to be Betty, the nanny. She pushed her blue-rimmed glasses up her nose.

"These little darlings were making such ruckus at the hotel, I decided to check us out early and come over in a cab before the manager paid us a visit."

Sergio scooped up the first child who made it to him and twirled her around, blowing a raspberry on her neck. "Hey, Laurel."

The girl squealed until he put her down and she promptly ran to the fence to watch the horses, peering through the lower rails. Laurel's twin hung back, her arms around Betty's leg, sneaking a sidelong look at Helen and Sergio.

"Come on, Lulu," Sergio said. "Don't I get a hug from my sweet girl?"

His gentle tone surprised Helen as the child walked hesitantly to Sergio with Betty's prompting. Sergio lifted Lucy slowly, much slower than he'd done with her sister, and embraced her. "It's okay. I'm here."

He touched her cheek. After a pause, Lucy spoke. "Hi, Daddy," she whispered before sticking the middle fingers of one hand in her mouth.

The two words caused Sergio's eyes to close in what appeared to be a combination of pain and pleasure as he cradled her to his chest. He must have felt Helen watching him and he looked her way. "She doesn't talk much. Probably because she got saddled with me as a parental figure at a sensitive time in her life. It took me a while to get the hang of it."

Saddled with Sergio, because Fiona had been run down. While Helen struggled to control the wild surge of grief and guilt, Betty spoke up.

"Lucy wouldn't eat dinner last night, or breakfast this morning," she said with a sigh. "She's got to be about half starved."

"Awww, Lulu," he murmured to her. "You gotta eat, buttercup, even when I'm not there, okay?"

Lucy didn't answer, just squeezed him tight, her free hands fingering his ears.

Helen fought a lump in her throat. "I'll have breakfast brought over. What would they like to eat?"

"Oh, that's so nice," Betty started, "but I brought some cereal."

"The chef makes a great funny-face pancake all the kids love, and scrambled eggs. Please," Helen said. "Oh, I'm sorry. You're probably wondering who I am." She quickly introduced herself. "It would… I mean, it's no trouble to arrange breakfast. There's also a buffet in the dining room."

Sergio shook his head. "I want to eat as a family, just us, until I can be sure Lucy's eating properly."

Just us. Helen swallowed. "So I'll have a tray made up then. Is that okay?" She waited to see if Sergio would reject that idea as well, if everything she offered would be rebuffed.

Betty looked to Sergio, and he paused, still cradling Lucy. "All right. That would be a special treat. Thank you."

She nodded, turning quickly to escape, but Laurel raced up to her, head tipped back, skin perfect as a flower petal in the new morning sunlight. “Can I ride a horse?” Her voice was high-pitched, face still bathed in wonder at the sight of the animals.

Helen looked into her eyes framed by long lashes, so very like her mother’s. Her voice failed her until Sergio drew close, still cradling Lucy.

“We’ll ride later, Laurel. Miss Helen has some things to do.”

Was he giving her a dismissal or a reprieve? She didn’t blame him for not wanting the girls to be around her. She could hardly stand the pain at having them close. It made her look at Sergio with new admiration. Somehow he’d put his anger and hurt aside to be Daddy to Lucy and Laurel. What sacrifices had he been forced to make?

“I’ll arrange for that breakfast,” she said, hurrying away. As she went, she felt Sergio’s gaze, heavy on her back and on her soul.

FIVE

Sergio played "horsie" with the girls while Betty had some overdue time to herself. This meant he spent a good half hour on his knees crawling around making neighing noises with Laurel and Lucy perched on his back. He'd perfected the art of bucking just enough to make them squeal but not quite enough to throw them off.

At first when he'd taken over as their guardian, he'd longed for the day when they weren't such delicate infants, but as they'd grown, he realized he had no idea how to play with small children. He'd eventually learned the secret. *Do whatever you can to put a smile on their faces.* That often meant leaving his dignity at the door, but he'd grown comfortable with that over the years. The only thing he stoutly refused to do was play with dolls. A grown man had to draw a line in the sand somewhere and pretending to make a plastic man doll with perfect hair chatter on was intolerable.

He'd tried hard to honor what he felt Fiona would have wanted, not to spoil them with toys and treats, but to lavish them with as much time as he could free up. There was never enough of that commodity, not with having to earn a living and the hours it took to track down the scant leads on his sister's murder, leads that had taken him nowhere until recently.

After he colored with the fat crayons Helen had left and made Play-Doh doughnuts and pretended to eat them, he considered what had happened in the woods. He'd already placed a call to the police and left a message.

He made a mental note to thank his pseudo informer, an interior designer, whose parents were family friends with his folks when they'd lived in Driftwood. He'd seen her business ad on Facebook while searching about all things Driftwood related, and contacted her after she'd announced she'd been awarded the contract to redecorate the Driftwood Police Department headquarters. Connections, he'd learned, were how a private eye got things done.

When he'd asked her to keep her ears open around the police department, she'd been surprisingly eager to tell him about Helen's arrival there the week before with Trish's mysterious note. She had no qualms about divulging private information, it seemed, and he was happy to overlook that transgression if it got him closer to nailing Fiona's killer. Amazing what a fly on the wall could take note of.

As soon as he got the girls settled in he would pay some important visits, the first to Chief Farraday and the second and third to Gavin Cutter and Justin Dover, the other two people who had been in the tunnels the night Trish O'Brian was murdered. None of the visits would involve Helen.

The doorbell rang, and he opened the door, surprised to find Helen standing there holding a tray, her face suffused with cotton-candy pink. She was dressed in an immaculate silk blouse and jeans that showed her long legs to advantage. There were no signs of their dangerous adventure in her outward appearance anymore. Gorgeous, he thought before he shut that unwanted observation down.

"You didn't have to bring it yourself," he finally said.

"I was out and about anyway." She offered him the tray.

He admired her pluck since he'd made his feelings perfectly clear. Laurel peeked around his leg. He realized he should have introduced them before. "Laurel, this is Miss Helen."

She smiled. "Hi, Laurel."

"We're gonna sit at the table for breakfast," Laurel said, looking at Sergio. "Can she sit too?"

"Oh, I've got to get back to the lodge. I'm…"

"Too busy," he said. He had not intended it to be a recrimination, but it might as well have been. Her flush deepened and he felt a prick of regret at paining her. She'd been kind and had gone out of her way, even if it was probably born of guilt. *Stop being a jerk, Sergio.*

"I…" Helen straightened and seemed to come to a decision. "I could stay for a minute," she said.

More courage. Her gleam of determination kicked his pulse up a notch.

Without warning, a blur of motion across the grass startled them all. Helen sighed at the approach of a white dog with crooked ears and amber eyes, a floppy cone stuck around his neck.

"Jingles," Helen said, "sit."

The dog promptly dropped into an awkward sit, legs sprawled out to one side. "I'm sorry. This is my brother's dog and he's here at the lodge while Liam is on his honeymoon. He doesn't know what to do with himself while Liam's gone. They're very bonded. Jingles is my guard dog at night. He bunks in my room in the main building."

Both girls were now peeking around Sergio's leg, staring at the strange sight.

"Owie?" Lucy said.

Helen smiled. "Oh, he got stuck in a barbed-wire fence and had to have stitches." She realized that was too difficult an explanation and added. "He wears that until his owie is better. He's supposed to get it off today."

Lucy blinked gravely.

"I'll keep him outside," Helen started, but Lucy was already scrambling past, plopping down on her knees to stroke Jingles's sides. The dog's eyes rolled blissfully.

Sergio shook his head. "Well I guess they're friends. He might as well come in too." He stood aside, and Lucy and Jingles made their way to the kitchen. Sergio hastily gathered up the stack of mangled *Ocean Life* magazines. He caught her amusement.

"The girls like to cut out the fish pictures. Sometimes they get started on that before I have a chance to read them." He added them to the pile of crumpled parenting magazines.

Helen smiled. "I remember cutting up my brother's comic book one time, and boy did I hear about that."

Laurel climbed up into the wooden chair, her sister beside her, and carefully tucked a paper napkin on her lap.

"What good manners," Helen said, sitting in the farthest chair away from Sergio.

He scooped Lucy up and set her in the seat next to him, smoothing the napkin for her. "I used to tuck the napkins under their chins, but Nanny Betty said that was uncouth."

Helen laughed. “Nanny was right.”

Laurel clasped her palms together. “Are you gonna say grace?”

Without missing a beat, Helen folded her hands and offered a simple prayer of thanksgiving. He folded his too, out of respect and because he was trying to raise them the way Fiona would have. He was trying to feel the surge of gratitude over the ever-present hum of stress and anger. “Thank you, Lord,” he echoed. “For bringing me here so I can find justice for my sister.”

He set to work cutting off a piece of the pancake, which was decorated with strawberry eyes and a banana slice mouth, and sticking it on the fork which he handed to Lucy. He was about to slide over and help Laurel, but Helen had gotten to it first. After slicing the pancake into neat bites, she poured a little puddle of syrup on the plate next to the pancake so Laurel could dip it in. He’d never thought of that. Instead he typically doused the goo over the whole pancake and cleaned up the sticky results later.

Helen poured coffee for the grown ups.

Sergio was pleased to note out of the corner of his eye that Lucy was eating with gusto.

“She’s got some developmental delays,” Sergio murmured quietly to Helen while the child remained absorbed in moving the pancake around her plate and Laurel chattered on. “I’m not exactly sure what all that means except things come more slowly to her and she isn’t growing as fast as her sister.”

Helen listened, sipping. They fell into an awkward silence.

“I called Chief Farraday,” she said while the children were piling in bites of pancake and giggling at Jingles.

“I did also. Left a message.”

"I told Mitch and Chad about it too."

Sergio drummed fingers on the table. "I've been thinking about the investigation all those years ago, Gavin and Justin were suspects for good reason."

Helen wiped her mouth. "I can't make myself believe either could do that to Trish."

"Maybe you can't see the bad in anyone."

Her look sharpened. "You sound like Liam. What you mean to say is I'm naive."

He didn't answer.

Helen cut another part of the pancake for Laurel and moved her glass of milk within reach. So smooth and natural. It had taken him dozens of spill cleanups to learn that toddlers couldn't reach too far without disaster. He didn't think she'd learned all these tricks from parenting magazines.

"I know you won't believe me, but my brother and I grew up fast—we had to. I'm more savvy about the evil in the world than you think. How could I not be after what happened to us in high school and later on to..." She broke off.

"Fiona," he finished quietly.

Helen pressed her lips in a firm line, but not until he'd seen the tremble there. For the first time, he imagined what it must have been like for her to be so close to two murders, and the initial one at such a tender age. Her phone buzzed, and she checked her text, her green eyes clouding. "Chief Farraday just arrived. He's waiting in the lobby for me. My desk clerk says he looks furious."

Sergio stood. "I'll ask Betty to watch the girls, and I'll come with you."

"I can handle it, Sergio. One thing I'm good at is managing lodge business."

"I'm sure you are, but I don't think this is exactly routine."

Her tone was chilly. "I'd rather you didn't. Like you said, you don't want me in your investigation, so I'll take care of this part myself and tell Farraday to direct all his questions to you. And, there's something you should probably know about a couple of the guests—"

He cut her off. "I won't make a scene and disturb the sacred ambiance of your lodge."

Her expression hardened, whatever she'd been about to tell him locked inside. "Yes, I love this lodge, Sergio. I won't deny that, and I love Gus and Ginny for trusting me to run it. They could have hired anyone, people with way more experience but they had faith in me and I work every day to make them proud. I'm not ashamed of that, but believe me…" Earnest grief edged into her tone now. "If I could go back in time, I would choose your sister over my duties in a heartbeat. I let her down…" Her pained gaze shifted to the children. "And I let them down." Anguish flashed as she dragged her eyes to his. "Does that make you feel better to hear me say it again?"

"No," he said, surprised that it was true. "Actually, it doesn't."

They both stood now, emotion crackling between them, the girls talking on, oblivious. The awkwardness stretched until she turned away.

"I will talk to the chief. I'm sure he'll want to have a word with you too, at some point," she said.

Sergio gave her a head start before he called for Betty and kissed each little girl on the top of her head. "No time like the present," he said. *Besides, maybe it's the perfect time to poke the bear.* He hoped it wouldn't make Helen's life harder, but he couldn't concern himself with that. Not now. It was his investigation, after all, if he could only convince her of that.

Helen strode into the lodge, where people were milling. Her clerks were doing their usual efficient jobs ushering the overnight guests and those visiting for the cattlemen's presentations into the spacious back area reserved for conferences and large events. She plucked a fallen napkin off the gleaming hardwood floor and discarded it. The lobby was perfect down to the last detail—the only way she'd allow it to be.

Farraday wasted no time, coming at her like a rocket closing in on a target. She moved away to a quiet corner where he started in.

"What are you trying to do? Get yourself killed? I told you to stay out of those tunnels."

"We weren't in the tunnels," she said firmly, "and we aren't the lawbreakers here."

"Your boy Kyle is," Sergio said as he joined them. Helen did her best to hide her annoyance.

Farraday's eyes slitted. "He's not 'my boy.' His name's Kyle Burnette. He's called me a few times to tell me when blockheads were out getting into the tunnels, and I've thanked him for that."

"Thanked him or paid him?" Sergio said.

"You're out of line," Farraday said. "He'll be cited for shooting at you."

"He should be arrested," Helen said calmly.

"He meant no harm."

Sergio was electric with irritation. "And what's his interest in the tunnels?"

Farraday blinked. "Just a good citizen."

"Uh-huh, and I'm the king of England," Sergio said.

A stream of people meandered past on their way to the conference room. Two men lingered close, one tall and dark, with thinning close-cut hair, gelled into a sheen, the other blond and shorter with a compact build. Helen's heart skidded.

Farraday eyed their approach as did Sergio who slid a look at Helen.

"These two are staying here at the lodge?" the chief asked.

She nodded. "They are both attending the cattlemen's convention." She took a deep breath. "Sergio, this is Gavin Cutter," she said, gesturing to the taller one, "and Justin Dover."

She saw the shock ripple over Sergio's face. He stared at Helen and she read the incredulity in his expression. He rubbed a hand over his chin, probably searching for composure.

Two prime suspects in Trish O'Brian's murder were indeed staying at the lodge. Part of her felt justified at his discomfort. She would have told him earlier if he'd been more cooperative.

Gavin extended a palm to Sergio; a gold band on his left ring finger caught the light. He still sported the same longish sideburns he'd been so proud of his senior year. "Name's Gavin Cutter. My wife and I own a cattle ranch just outside of town." He waved to a woman with a mane of curly hair, stepping into the elevator before the doors slid shut. "There she is. That's Dee."

The other man shook hands, as well. "Justin Dover." His blond brows drew together. "I'm sorry. I've heard… I mean… I can't actually believe it, but…"

"I can," Gavin said. His dark eyes were shadowed

with fatigue, she noticed. “The whole high school thing is rearing its ugly head again.”

Justin groaned. “Will it ever be over?”

“Not until Trish O’Brian’s killer is caught,” Sergio said.

Both men stiffened. Gavin’s eyes narrowed. “I’m not sure what your interest is in all this, but we were both cleared of that crime.”

“My interest?” Sergio said. “Easy. It seems that whoever killed Trish O’Brian might have also murdered my sister, Fiona Ross. I’m here to find out the truth about that.”

“You’re Fiona’s brother?” Gavin’s mouth pinched into a tight line. “I saw you around in high school a few times, but I don’t think we ever formally met. You graduated a couple years ahead of us. I was so sorry to hear about Fiona’s death, we both were, but listen to me. I believe to this day that there was someone else in those tunnels that night who killed Trish.”

“And you had nothing to do with it?” Sergio’s question reeked of disbelief.

“My whole life stalled after what happened,” Gavin snarled, “but now I’m finally restarting it. I’ve got a wife and a baby on the way and my ranch is edging into the black. Remember that when you’re stirring the pot around here. People’s reputations are on the line.”

“Only the guilty will pay,” Sergio said. “I promise.”

Justin sighed. “The police found us innocent.”

Helen searched Farraday’s face but saw no reaction there.

“Not being charged with a crime doesn’t necessarily mean someone’s innocent,” Sergio said.

Gavin’s hands tightened into fists.

Justin shook his head and sighed. "There will always be people in this town who think we killed her." He looked at Helen, his gray eyes troubled. "You remember what that felt like when the cops were looking at you?"

Helen gulped. She did. If she and Fiona hadn't gotten lost and exited a tunnel completely on the other side of the forest, they would have been, and briefly were, suspects too.

"I'll help in any way I can." Justin shot a look at Gavin who nodded grudgingly. "We'll both cooperate fully. Fiona was our friend too and if her murder is linked to Trish's we want to help you sort that out, but just be careful, okay? We shouldn't have to pay all over again for something we didn't do."

When Sergio didn't answer, Helen nodded. "The next session is starting in the conference room."

Gavin and Justin headed away.

Farraday rolled one shoulder as if he felt a pain there. "Good reminder. Don't mess up people's lives trying to play at being detectives."

"Do I look like I'm playing?" Sergio spoke softly, but his words were knife edged.

Farraday turned abruptly and strode away. Helen watched him pass by a woman with a pixie cut of flame-colored hair. She was bundled in a leather coat, striding toward the conference room. Her cheeks were heavily freckled.

That red hair. Those freckles. They struck Helen in such a familiar way that she did a double take, but the woman had passed by without acknowledging her. A stranger. She must be.

"What?" Sergio said, noting her interest.

"Oh, nothing. Someone I thought I knew."

Forget the past, Helen. You've got a job to do right now. With Liam's wife Maggie, her new cook, away for her honeymoon, she needed to check in with Tiny, the man she'd borrowed from the local Chuckwagon Restaurant to fill in. There were ingredient spreadsheets to go over, employee schedules to finalize. Part of her longed for the steadying element of neat columns and tidy sums.

"I've got to go," she told Sergio. Though she had the feeling he wanted to talk to her about Gavin and Justin, it would have to wait.

Put him off like you did to Fiona? Guilt stabbed through her but when she looked around to catch Sergio, he'd already left.

It wasn't until well after eleven that evening that Helen trudged up the stairs to her room, her private oasis. It was the only place she could escape the demands of the lodge. Her body was exhausted, but her mind was temporarily satisfied.

Tiny had done a stellar job preparing vats of cowboy chili, his famous corn bread and pans of peach cobbler which satisfied the convention goers and the regular patrons alike. The combination of Tiny's cooking talent and her behind-the-scenes planning had paid off. Each step sapped her energy further. Tired as she was, she could not stop the thoughts from flailing around in her head about Fiona's and Trish's untimely deaths. Not just deaths, murders. Farraday thought she and Sergio were playing detective games, but there was nothing trivial about the stakes.

The capture of Trish's murderer.

Unmasking Fiona's killer.

And the reputations of two men who had already

had their lives ripped apart. Justin's words echoed in her mind.

We shouldn't have to pay all over again for something we didn't do.

She used her key, pushing the heavy wood door ajar, waiting for the exuberant greeting from Jingles. Mitch had taken him to the vet to have his sutures checked and was to have secured the dog in her room while she completed her evening rounds.

The dog did not come.

"Jingles?" she called, reaching for the light switch. She flicked it twice with no results. A power outage? Not unheard of since the main building hadn't been remodeled like the more modernized cabins. The biggest improvement had been installing key card readers on the lobby doors which gave her more comfort about lodge security. That modernization hadn't been applied to her own room. The Best for the Guests, was her motto. Perhaps Mitch had kept Jingles on the ranch for some reason.

She was reaching for her phone to activate the flashlight when something moved in the darkness, something that was not canine, but human.

SIX

Sergio walked, hands pocketed against the winter night. The darkness reminded him of diving into cold, sunless layers of a lake with only the pulse of his regulator sounding in his ears. Lake diving was the best, sinking into that void, searching for mummified old wood tree trunks with superfine grain that might be worth thousands. The money was great, the excitement satisfying, but what he missed most was that quiet. He'd always figured diving was one of the greatest blessings of his life, until he'd had to give it up for a different blessing, or two to be more precise. Now his quiet was virtually nonexistent, and he still craved it.

The girls were sleeping in peaceful oblivion, after plenty of bedtime stories and drinks of water. What in the world made them so thirsty right at bedtime? After they'd settled, he'd been making notes in his file, using his PI privileges to pull city and county records for Gavin and Justin, run license checks on both of them, and peruse articles about Trish's murder.

His eyes still burned from hours staring at the screen, soaking in the familiar details, hoping for some sort of new revelation. Gavin and Justin maintained steadfastly that after they entered the tunnels and split up, they'd each assumed Trish had gone with Fiona and Helen. Only when they'd finally regrouped had they discovered her missing. Helen and Fiona had exited a different way, together, which put them a good thirty minutes from the tunnel entrance. The women had tried to place a cell phone call at that time, which provided proof of their location.

As he strolled along, he ran through more facts in his mind. The copious amounts of water dumped by a storm that night in the tunnels had washed the crime scene clean, according to Farraday who was a sergeant then. At the time of Trish's death, he was in his midforties, having been with the Driftwood Police Department after a transfer from a much bigger department in New Mexico. Farraday and his subordinate Frank Higgins had found no fingerprints on the wet stone. No hairs or fibers left behind, just the coroner's conclusion that Trish had been hit with a blunt object which was not discovered at the scene.

Had Trish stumbled upon someone hiding out there in those tunnels as Gavin suggested? If so, that strengthened Farraday's opinion that Trish's death and Fiona's were unrelated. And the shooter whom Sergio had found little information about, Kyle Burnette? Was his attack purely coincidental? He could not force himself to believe it.

Is it because you're making yourself feel better by believing you can bring her justice?

Sergio realized he'd been walking long enough to have circled around to the back of the lodge. The place was lit with the soft glow of some artfully placed lamps, just enough to illuminate the pathways and outline the roofs. At this hour all was quiet, save for the wind in the trees. Even the patio area with its massive stone firepit was deserted. He made up his mind to return to the cabin and try again to grab hold of the ever-elusive sleep, when he heard the rustle of leaves. He froze.

Too big for a raccoon, whatever it could be was making no effort at stealth. He paused and waited. A flash of white moved behind the leaves.

"Jingles?" he called.

The dog burst through the foliage, tail wagging so hard his hind end shimmied back and forth. Sergio dropped to one knee and scrubbed the dog behind the ears. "What are you doing out here? Did you escape the lodge?"

Jingles is my guard dog at night. He bunks in my room.

Sergio considered. The dog had followed Helen out to the cottage for her breakfast delivery that morning, glued to her side. How could he have gotten out of Helen's room and left the lodge altogether? Jingles whined and danced up and down in agitation.

A wash of cold slithered through Sergio's stomach. Pulling his key card from his pocket, he ran to the side entrance and jammed it into the card reader. Wrenching open the door, he fought for calm. It was probably nothing, the wandering of a naughty dog. He dialed Helen's cell phone. One ring, two. No answer.

The night desk clerk gave him a startled look. Her name tag read Evonne. "Can I help you, sir?"

He jogged to her. "I found Jingles outside."

The clerk frowned. "Really? I know Mitch put him in her room an hour or so ago. Jingles was happy to be out of that horrible cone. How did he get out?"

"Call her," he said. "Please."

The clerk nodded and dialed a phone. The seconds ticked away, and Sergio's nerves fired into full gear.

"She doesn't answer, sir. Shall I…?"

"How do I get to her room?"

"I…"

"How?" he demanded. "She's in trouble."

The urgency in his tone must have convinced her. She pointed to the stairwell behind the front desk. He skirted the counter and took the stairs two at a time, Jingles charging up behind him.

Helen blinked awake, her brain spongy and uncooperative. She realized slowly, very slowly, that she was lying on the floor, facing the wall. Her arm stung, and an empty hypodermic needle lay between her sprawled legs and a cherrywood table.

Drugged.

Reality intruded into her fogged mind. She'd come through the door, been stabbed with a hypodermic, giving her attacker ample time to rifle through her belongings. She'd struggled, but the drug overtook her and her attacker had been strong. Her limbs were cement, head heavy as if her neck could hardly sustain the weight. Dumbly she stared at the soft green wall, willing her senses to come back online. *Move. Get away. Hurry.* But her body would not obey.

She heard the sound of drawers being stealthily opened in the adjoining room and she realized the intruder was in her bedroom, going through her wardrobe. He or she must have waited until Evonne was away from her post behind the check-in desk to sneak up the stairs and break into the room.

Phone. She had to get to her phone and call the front desk, text Sergio, something. Straining to the point where her teeth ground together, she moved her hand inch by inch to her pocket. Stomach diving, she realized her phone was not there. Whoever had drugged her had taken it away. What could they want? Why risk sneaking into her room in such a public place? What could she have that might make the audacious act worth the risk?

A soft squeak made her cold with terror.

The faint vibration of footsteps across the bedroom floor told her the attacker was returning. Should she lie still? Pretend to be unconscious and let him or her search until they were satisfied? The idea of rendering herself completely helpless sickened her.

Move, move, her brain screamed. *Get out.* In a matter of moments the intruder would join her in the front room.

She managed to flop toward the door. If she could just get to the stairs and scoot down, tumble even, anything that would get her to safety.

Another few inches of wriggling and she was on her hands and knees, nearer the door, arms trembling with the effort. Her legs would not support her so she would have to drag herself with her arms.

Hurry.

Though she could not command herself to look toward the bedroom, her palms picked up the feel of feet moving quickly across the wood floor. He was coming. She would not make it.

Scream, she told herself.

She'd just opened her mouth when the intruder grabbed her hair, shoved her own pillow on the floor in front of her and pressed her head into the fabric. The down sealed off her air, suffocating her in a cloud of softness.

She struggled and bucked against the hands that held

her, but her drugged body would not respond. No air, a slow suffocating death. She heard a humming in her ears and she knew she was losing the fight.

With everything in her she wriggled, trying to turn her face to one side, but fingers imprisoned her head, sealing her mouth and nose against the fabric.

How could it end here? On her beloved lodge floor? With her own pillow? Panic and prayer tumbled inside her. One more breath, just stay alive for one more moment. But she could not fight against the weight that forced her to confront her own death. Darkness nibbled the edges of her consciousness.

She wanted to cry, but she was motionless, locked in a silent scream. Blackness coalesced into an ocean. She tried once more to suck in a desperate breath. There was a muffled shout from the hallway, and her attacker let go. Her front door was flung open and she heard the scampering of nails across the floor.

Someone was turning her over.

"Helen," came the voice, almost pleading. She blinked, still fighting for air as Sergio's face swam into view. He clutched her upper arms. "It's okay. Catch your breath. In and out, that's good."

Jingles whined and licked her cheek. Helen saw Evonne, stricken and terrified, peering down. "Oh, Helen. Someone snuck up here when I was away from the desk. I am so sorry."

Helen tried to speak.

"The ambulance is on its way." Evonne held up a hand and gave her a shaky smile. "No sirens, I know. Nothing to upset the guests."

Helen felt the burning in her lungs subside. "Who…?" she whispered.

"I don't know," Sergio said. "Whoever it was climbed out your bedroom window and down the drainpipe. Dropped your phone on the floor. Cops are en route, for what it's worth. Do you want me to call your brothers?"

She tried to answer, but instead she felt the swell of hot tears.

"It's okay," he said, with surprising gentleness, stroking his fingers over her hair. "I'll take care of you."

She closed her eyes. Of all the people whom she would imagine coming to save her, this man was surely at the bottom of the list. Yet there he was, holding her hand, keeping Jingles from crawling on top of her, talking to the paramedics when they arrived and insisting on sitting next to her in the ambulance. It was both puzzling and humiliating.

She was grateful that the medics and hotel staff were discreet, bundling her out the side door without alarming the guests or creating a scene. The next hour was a blur of doctors buzzing around her, and after a while, Mitch and Chad arriving along with Ginny and Gus. Sergio must have called them. She did not spot him amidst the cowboys arranged around her bedside. Her throat burned and her head throbbed, but there would be no lasting damage, according to the doctors.

She didn't want to entertain the thought that kept biting at her, but finally she could ignore it no longer.

"I surprised whoever it was." She gulped. "I wasn't strong enough to get away."

Ginny squeezed her hand. "You were drugged. Doctor said it was xylazine."

"A horse sedative," Mitch said. "But fortunately it was a small dose. Police are processing the evidence. Looks like someone was searching for something. They picked the lock when there was no one behind the registration desk. Evonne said she left her post for a half hour to check in a delivery to the kitchen."

"I almost got a look at their face." She shuddered.

"And whoever it was couldn't let that happen. I'm guessing they brought the sedative in case they were discovered. When you tried to scream..." It was Sergio standing in the corner, arms crossed. "He or she panicked and tried to smother you."

"Man or woman?" Chad asked.

"I don't know. I didn't see a thing. I feel like an idiot walking right in like that."

"Why should you worry about your safety in your own bedroom?" Ginny's touch grew tight on her arm. "You have to come stay with us. At least until this mess is resolved."

Helen sat up higher on the pillows. "I am not letting anyone run me out of the lodge. We're packed with guests, and I need to get back there."

"Police aren't done," Sergio pointed out. "You can't sleep there tonight anyway, maybe tomorrow too."

"And the doctor said you are to take two days off. Period," Aunt Ginny said. "Before you protest, I already spoke to Tiny and Evonne. I told them we're bringing in more help, some of my friends from a hotel in Sand Dune who are happy to step in until you return. It's handled."

"But the breakfast..."

Ginny shook her head. "Quiches are prepped for the oven, per Tiny."

"The AV equipment they need for their presentation will..."

"Be set up in a matter of hours," Ginny finished.

"I just can't…" Helen started, feeling the prick of helpless tears.

"Helen," Uncle Gus said, the softness in his tone making her eyes fill even more. "Listen to Ginny, sweetheart."

"All right. Two days. Then I'm going back to the lodge. I'll get another lock on the door and Jingles will stay with me."

"He didn't do such a great job as your guard dog," Mitch pointed out.

"The intruder let him outside. Jingles was probably thinking it was a fun game at first." Helen bit her lip. "He's such a friendly dog, too friendly, especially with women."

Women. Sergio flicked a look at her.

"Well he's learned a trick or two, I think," Mitch said. "I had to drop him at the ranch with Jane because he wouldn't stop barking when they loaded you into the ambulance."

Helen groaned. "How embarrassing."

"Scary, is more like it," Ginny said. "Someone breaking into your room. It makes me furious to think about it."

Helen swallowed hard, the memory of suffocating almost overwhelming her. "Could it be the same man who shot at us? Kyle Burnette?"

"I'm asking around to see if someone can put him at the scene," Mitch said. "Nothing so far. Did you see him anywhere about the lodge?"

She shook her head which jarred her nerves. "No." Recalling it all made her stomach tighten. "I would have been dead if Sergio hadn't found me."

"So we should be thanking him or something?" Chad snapped. "He's the reason you're at risk."

Sergio cocked his head. “How do you figure that?”

“You’ve been stirring up trouble all over town. Taking her to the tunnels and getting shot at? What kind of an idea was that?” Helen had not seen Chad angry very often, but now his eyes snapped with fury.

“Mine,” Helen said firmly. “It was my idea.”

“Well you should have come and gotten me or Mitch,” Chad said, a vein jumping in his jaw. “Not him.”

Helen pressed a hand to her temple and groaned.

“It’s not the time for this,” Ginny said. “All of you simmer down right now or you’re leaving this room, do you understand me?”

No one answered.

“I said,” she repeated, “Do you understand me?”

“Yes, ma’am,” Mitch, Chad and Gus said simultaneously. Sergio nodded his agreement.

“All right then.” Ginny smoothed Helen’s blanket. “We’re going to tell Liam, by the way.” She stopped Helen’s protest with a firm shake of her head. “Maggie’s gotten food poisoning and she’s sick as all get-out, but the doctors said she’ll be fine. I got that message this morning. As soon as she’s better, we’re going to tell him.”

She rolled her eyes. “He’s going to fly back here like a missile.”

“And explode just as likely,” said Chad. “But there’s no choice.”

They were right. It would be crushing for Liam to know she was in trouble and he hadn’t been told. Helen sighed. Just what she needed. Another protective male added to the mix. Recalling the smothering pressure of a pillow, she suppressed a shiver. As much as she didn’t want to admit it, she was scared.

Across the room Sergio’s eyes met hers. She also

didn't want to acknowledge that it made her feel better somehow, to have him there.

Why was her world suddenly turned upside down? Sergio wasn't a friend; as a matter of fact he thought of her as the enemy. Yet as she watched him, his expression had lost some of its granite edge.

Enemy or not, Sergio had saved her life.

How exactly was she supposed to handle that unsettling fact?

SEVEN

The tension escalated when Farraday entered the room. It was now shifting from night to a gray morning and drops of rain clung to his uniform jacket. Sergio thought idly that he'd better help Betty entertain the girls if it was going to be a rainy day. Again he felt torn between the demands of fatherhood and his job. His brain wanted to go dig into the most minute details of what had just happened to Helen, to get his hands on her attacker without a moment's delay. His heart brought him back to his girls. Was that what parenting was about? The constant tension of not knowing what to prioritize and when?

Farraday was solicitous, asking Helen about her condition before he got down to business. He eyed the visitors in the room. "May I speak to Helen privately?"

"No," came the unified response from Mitch, Chad, Sergio and Gus.

He thought Aunt Ginny hid a smile. Sergio knew that as a cop, Farraday could force the issue, but he was smart enough to be savvy about catching flies with honey instead of vinegar.

"Now do you believe me that there's something very wrong going on here?" Helen said.

"What I know is that someone attacked you in your room, Miss Pike. At this point there's no way to ascertain if it's connected to anything from the past."

Sergio strove for calm. "So you figure it's just a coincidence that she was almost killed after asking you to reopen the Trish O'Brian case?"

"We're investigating. That's all I'm prepared to say right now." He asked Helen some questions, most of which she could not answer.

Sergio soaked in the details.

"Looks like the perp picked the lock on your door, probably let your dog down the back stairs and outside. We found a beef jerky wrapper."

Helen grimaced. "Don't tell Liam that Jingles was bought off by beef jerky."

"Since your security cameras cover the parking lot only, there was no footage of anyone entering or exiting." He paused. "No cars coming or going either."

Mitch raised a brow. "It might have been a guest then? Someone staying at the lodge?"

"It's conceivable it was a conference attendee staying on-site or perhaps a daytime guest who swiped a key card and snuck in the back through the woods."

Mitch nodded. "Interviews?"

"We've talked to the staff, the night custodian, etc., and no one saw anyone skulking around. Guy wore gloves probably. No prints that we've found except Helen's and housekeeping." Sergio knew the meat and potatoes of it was coming.

Farraday cleared his throat. "I spoke with Justin Dover and Gavin Cutter. They both said they were in their rooms. I have no way to prove nor disprove their statements, but if it means anything, they both appeared completely shocked."

Appearances could be deceiving.

"But both could have had easy access to a horse sedative," Uncle Gus put in.

Helen shook her head. "Along with everyone else at the convention. They're all ranchers with horses or they're in a related business anyway."

"We're running backgrounds on all the guests, but that's going to take a while."

"The woman," Sergio said, catching Helen's eye. "The one you took a second look at yesterday. Who was she?"

Helen frowned. "I'm not positive. I didn't get a chance to ask my staff."

"But who did you think she was?" he said.

"Something about her caught my attention. I could have been wrong, I mean, I haven't seen her in years and we were so young."

"Who?" Sergio pressed, as gently as he could.

"Those freckles stood out to me. I know, I knew another woman with freckles like that."

This time it was Chad who chimed in. "Helen, just spit it out. Who did she remind you of?"

"Allyson O'Brian, Trish O'Brian's sister."

Sergio hadn't seen that coming. Judging by the look on the other's faces, they hadn't either.

Farraday finally spoke. "Allyson lives with her folks in Denton about twenty minutes north. She's pretty big into dressage, I hear."

Ginny raised an eyebrow. "But not ranching?"

He shook his head.

"Then why would she be at the lodge for a cattlemen's convention?" Ginny said.

Helen plucked at her blanket with nervous fingers. "There are breeders there. Some of them deal in dressage horses."

Farraday nodded. "She wasn't on the list of overnight guests, nor was she registered for the convention. I'll go pay her a visit. Could be a completely innocent reason she was on-site."

Sergio didn't reply. There were now three people in or around the lodge intimately connected with Trish O'Brian. One of them must know something that would help crack the case wide-open. Farraday might ask some questions, but Sergio intended to do everything he could to move the case forward.

The situation was growing steadily more dangerous, deadly even. He recalled rolling Helen off the pillow, praying he wasn't too late. What if he'd stopped to call her cell one more time? Or phone Mitch? He allowed himself exactly two seconds to consider how else things might have turned out for Helen if he had made a different decision.

Throat gone dry, he wondered how much time they had before someone tried to end Helen's investigations once and for all. It was another excellent reason why he needed to keep her far away from any future work on the case.

And then maybe he could get her off his mind once and for all.

Helen stayed in the hospital until the following afternoon before she was bundled along to Gus and Ginny's. She'd texted and called Evonne so often that Ginny threatened to take away her phone. Everything seemed to be perfectly under control. In spite of a headache and a sore throat that was not eased by Ginny's chicken and dumplings, Helen felt perfectly able, and downright anxious, to work. Yet her bruised arm where the needle had stabbed her was a stark reminder of what might have been. She insisted on sitting up in the leather armchair in the living room where she could see out the wide windows across the sweep of green to the wave-tossed Pacific when she wasn't checking on invoices and returning emails on her laptop.

Mitch and Chad had gone off to tend to the herd of grass-fed cattle that made their home on the vast acreage of the Roughwater. Jane arrived with magazines in one hand and her young son Charlie in the other. Helen kissed Charlie when he hugged her around the neck.

"Here is something to read while you recuperate," Jane said.

"Thank you, but it's hard to concentrate on anything."

Jane squeezed her shoulder. "I know what that's like."

She did too. Helen often marveled at the courage Jane had shown, running from her serial-killer ex-husband, living like a fugitive herself to keep Charlie safe. She eyed the little boy as he chattered on about their cat who slept on a pink pillow in Charlie's room.

She smiled as his story unfolded, thinking that he would get along well with Lucy and Laurel. She was about to tell Jane about the girls when her cell phone rang. Jane motioned that she would take Charlie into the other room to allow her some privacy.

"Helen." Gavin's deep voice made her start. "I heard about what happened. I'm so sorry. Are you okay? Can I do anything for you?"

"I'm fine. It's so nice of you to call." They kept up the small talk for a while until Helen decided it was time to do a little sleuthing of her own, no matter what her brothers and Sergio thought. "Gavin, did you know Allyson O'Brian was visiting the lodge yesterday?"

There was a long pause. "Yes. To be honest, I avoided her."

"May I ask why?"

He hesitated. "We never got along well in high school. And the actual truth is, she was pesky, the kid sister always trying to be a part of our group. Trish tried to avoid her whenever possible, and I wasn't exactly warm and welcoming. She…" he cleared his throat. "She wanted to come along, that night, the night we went to the tunnels. Did you know that?"

Helen's heart thudded at the memory. "No, I didn't. I was pretty wrapped up in myself, back then."

"Trish lied to Allyson, told her we were going to the movies and ditched her. She found out and called Trish, throwing an awful fit. I always felt bad about that, especially, you know, considering things happened the way they did. I mean, it was better that she wasn't there, but I'm sure it was a double whammy. First her sister lied to her and they fought and second someone murdered Trish the same night. Everyone's life changed back then."

There was such sadness in his voice, that mirrored her own. They'd lost their childhood that night, all of them, any last vestiges of innocence had been sucked away by those dark tunnels.

"I didn't realize. Thank you for telling me."

"Sometimes I feel like I'm imprisoned by that day and I can't escape no matter how much time passes."

"Me too."

The silence spooled into awkwardness. "Did I tell you my wife is expecting? It will be our first. It's a girl."

"That's wonderful, Gavin. I'm so pleased for you."

"I've finally allowed myself to start believing that past is all behind me and now it's rearing up again." He paused. "Do you think what happened to you is because you've been looking into Trish's death?"

"I don't know. I'm going to message Allyson to see if I can meet with her. Maybe she can shed some light."

"Could be you're finally getting close to the truth, after all these years. How amazing would it be to know who did it, and have the suspicions finally dead and gone?" His voice hitched. "That's just false hope. I don't really think the answer will ever be known. I don't want my wife and daughter to suffer because of what happened all those years ago, and I also don't want the truth at the expense of your safety or anyone's. There's been too much death here in this town already."

Too much death. "I feel that way too."

"Leave it alone, Helen. For your own good."

Was Gavin a concerned friend? Or was he warning her for another reason? Suddenly, the room felt cold. "Thanks for calling."

"No problem. We can talk when you come back to the lodge."

Was there something else he wanted to say?

"Sure. I'll see you soon." He disconnected.

Evonne texted her a message that Farraday was requesting to talk to her.

She texted back. "I'm hoping to see Allyson O'Brian sometime today. Tell him I'll call him after that."

She put the phone down and rested her pounding head on the supple leather. *Leave it alone...for your own good.* She must have dozed off, startled awake at the scrape of a chair. Sergio sat across from her, those rich brown eyes searching her face.

"Sorry I woke you," he said.

"That's okay." For some reason it made her feel strange to see him there, intense, filled with suppressed energy.

"How are the girls?"

"Doing well. I snuck home after the hospital and we played Play-Doh. Whoever invented that stuff was brilliant, but it should come with instructions for how to get it out of hair."

She giggled, picturing Sergio rolling out Play-Doh. "As a matter of fact," she reached over and plucked a blob of yellow from the hair at his temple. Her fingers grazed the strong line of his chin. He jerked, as if he'd gotten a shock.

"Oh, uh, thanks." He pulled a piece of paper from his pocket. "I thought you'd enjoy this."

She peered at the scribbled crayon.

"It's Jingles," he said. "Lucy drew it for you."

She could pick out the fat body and four stick legs. "Oh, I see it now. But…does he have two heads?"

"I think she's confused about his cone."

She laughed, then grimaced. "I love it. Thank you for bringing it." She looked more carefully. "But you didn't come over here just to deliver that, did you?"

He shrugged. "No. In all honesty, I searched the cabin again. Chad and Mitch helped me."

Her pulse revved. "Did you find anything?"

"No. Nothing, nothing to shed any further light on the paper you found."

Trish. Proof.

Find out who still has theirs.

Helen rubbed at her temple. "If we could just figure out what she was looking for. Whatever it is, the person who broke into my room thinks I've got it."

He got up and stared out the window. "Something that connects you and Fiona and Trish. A diary?"

"None of us kept one, to my knowledge. I should have asked Gavin when he called." She recapped the phone conversation for him. "He…he thinks I should let things go, not ask any more questions."

Sergio's eyes narrowed and she knew he was thinking the same thing she was about Gavin's motives. "Good to know about that tension between Trish and Allyson. I ran some reports on both Gavin and Justin. Nothing stands out. Gavin went into the army after high school and served without incident, worked in private industry until three years ago when he moved back to help run his parents' ranch which he's since inherited. Justin relocated down south and did some junior college. He's worked mostly in sales. Married and divorced, no kids, lives in a condo not far from here. Didn't find much on Allyson either. She went away to college, but only lasted six months before she moved home to live with her parents in their new place. Doesn't seem to have a job that I can discern, lives on Mom and Dad's dime. She's never married, though she's been in plenty of relationships, from what I can tell."

Helen winced at the way Sergio had boiled down their lives into a series of statements. "It wasn't easy for any of them to move past what happened, I'm sure."

Sergio shrugged. "You did."

"In some ways." She looked away. All the new developments made her wonder if she'd really left it all behind or merely covered it up with other things.

He didn't seem to notice. "I'm not feeling too confident that Farraday is going to ask Allyson the right questions, so I'm going to pay her a visit."

"When?"

"Now."

She threw off the blanket. "I'm coming too."

"No, you're not."

"Watch me."

He faced her, arms folded across his chest. "You're on doctor's orders to rest."

Helen stood and tipped her chin to look him full-on. "I was almost killed in my own bedroom. I'm knee-deep in this investigation whether you like it or not."

"You've got a lodge to run."

A lodge to run. It hit her like an arrow and she wondered if he'd meant it to. "Don't throw that in my face, Sergio. I was too busy before to help your sister. If there's a chance now to find out who killed her, then I'm going to stay on it like a tick on a coonhound, as Liam would say."

He stared, then smiled. The smile softened the hard lines of his face, transforming him into a gentler version of himself, like an ice sculpture that had just begun to melt away the jagged edges. For a split second she wished she could see more of the other Sergio, the one that didn't look at her through the lens of what he'd lost.

"Believe it or not, I wasn't heaping blame on you. We've both suffered because of what happened."

She blinked, throat suddenly clogged, unsure what to say.

"All right," he said. "If you're going to be all stubborn about it, I'll drive us to Allyson's, but we'd better scram before your brothers get back or they're liable to lasso you to a chair."

"I'd like to see them try," she said.

He quirked an eyebrow. "Well they'd definitely not hesitate to tie me to a fence post."

"Now that is a fact."

His smile slowly faded, replaced by an enigmatic expression. Tenderness? Concern? "I can't let anything happen to you."

"It won't," she said lightly. "Let's go before our absence is noted." She was relieved to be back on solid ground, but his words still danced through her.

I can't let anything happen to you.

She wasn't sure what to make of his remark, or the reaction it awakened, so she filed away the shaky feelings to examine more closely when she was safely alone.

EIGHT

Helen strode so quickly to Sergio's car that she was climbing inside before he got a chance to open the door for her. It was probably just as well to speed along their departure before Gus or Ginny intervened, Helen knew. She picked up a purple stuffed rabbit from the passenger seat.

"Yours?" she quipped.

"Of course not. It's Laurel's. Mine's blue."

She could not resist a chuckle. "You'd get along great with my brother Liam. He's quite the jokester."

"Something tells me he's not going to enjoy my company much when he's told what's happened to you on my watch."

She started. "Your watch?" She regarded him as he squirmed on the seat.

"I meant that...well, I mean, I feel responsible for you."

"Why would you feel that way?"

He fiddled with his keys. "My sister loved you."

"I loved her too." She blinked back a sudden gush of tears. It was as if a floodgate opened inside her and the truth spilled out. "I am so sorry about what happened, Sergio. If only I could go back in time..."

"I've said the same thing to myself," he said gruffly. "I should have checked in with her more, called, but I was too busy, occupied with my work or just larking around the planet, entertaining myself instead of being more involved."

Pain lanced through her. "But your busyness didn't cause her death. Mine did."

He paused for a moment before answering. "Helen, the guy driving the car who ran her over is responsible."

"You don't have to let me off the hook. I never will."

To her surprise, he reached out and took her hand. His fingers were long and calloused.

"I don't think that's what Fiona would have wanted." She wasn't sure why his tone sounded suddenly kinder. Probably just knowing the trauma she had recently experienced, the terrible fright she'd had which had probably rattled him plenty too.

"Fiona didn't hold grudges," he said.

"But you do," Helen said softly, pulling away. "And you've got the right to."

Instead of answering, he reached for the ignition. He looked as though he was wrestling with a thought when a compact car pulled onto the property, Justin Dover behind the wheel.

"What does he want?" Sergio wondered aloud. Helen rolled down her window. Justin walked over to the SUV and handed Helen a bunch of yellow daisies wrapped in cellophane.

"These are for you. I can't believe what happened, and right there under our noses. Are you okay?" His hair was a darker blond than it had been in high school, thinning a bit at the temples. He was still fit, as though he'd kept the hummingbird metabolism he'd enjoyed as a teen. He bent so he could see into the car, nodding at Sergio.

"Thank you for the flowers, Justin. That's so kind of you. I'm fine—a headache is the only souvenir. Sergio got to me in time."

Justin winced. "It's terrible. The desk clerk told me you were off for a few days to recuperate." He looked puzzled and rubbed his brow, the black stone in his ring catching the sunlight. They used to tease him that he was ready for Hollywood with his blond hair, stylish jeans and the ring with the ostentatious red stone he used to favor as a high school senior.

He caught her looking at it and laughed. "Some Mr. Hollywood I turned out to be, huh? A salesman in a Podunk town with an ex-wife and a rattletrap pickup."

She blushed. "You always were a snappy dresser. I hope we didn't harass you too much with our ribbing."

"Nah. I could dish it out as well as take it. What was your nickname?"

"Bookworm."

He laughed. "That's right. I guess we all had our quirks."

"Yes, we sure did." Flashy Justin, Gavin the jock, Helen, studious and quiet, Trish the cheerleader and Fiona, the outgoing student body president. Where had those days gone?

"Did I catch you on your way out?" he said.

"We're…" Helen started.

Sergio cut her off. "Yes, on the way out."

"Um, we're running a quick errand, is all," Helen added to soften Sergio's blunt brushoff.

"Oh. Okay. I won't take up your time." He frowned

and shook his head. “I’ve just been thinking about some of Farraday’s questions.”

Sergio leaned closer to see Justin more clearly, his hard shoulder touching hers. “Which ones?”

“He surprised me when he asked if anyone at the lodge had also been in town when Fiona was killed. It struck me odd, is all.”

Sergio frowned. “Did you make any connections between those two events?”

Justin grimaced. “No. I had no idea the two things could be related. And now Farraday thinks your attack might actually be connected to what happened to Trish or Fiona?”

“We’re not sure,” Helen said.

Justin whistled. “This is mind-blowing. After all these years. I lost hope that there would ever be progress on Trish’s case. It went cold so long ago. Now to find out there may be a link to another death…and your attack. It’s unbelievable.”

“Who do you think killed Trish?” If Sergio intended the question to startle, it seemed to have worked. Justin’s expression went slack.

He shook his head. “If you only knew how long I’ve mulled that over. I just don’t know.”

“What does your gut say? You were there, you and Gavin and Helen, along with my sister,” Sergio said. “Who do you think killed her?”

Justin’s mouth opened, and he started to speak, then stopped.

“I know it wasn’t any of us. Gavin and I were together except for a half hour or so, but I never thought he did it for a second. He was only aggressive during basketball games.” Justin offered a crooked smile. “I took an elbow or two and got a black eye once, but he didn't have much of a temper off the court. Just don't mess with his lay-ups."

"He was dating Trish. Did they love each other?"

Justin blew out a breath. "Love is a strong word. I mean, we were high schoolers, right?"

Sergio didn't return his smile. "That doesn't answer my question."

"He liked her I guess, and maybe she felt a little stronger on her end, is all. He just wanted to hang out, you know? Trish thought it was a sign of something more lasting."

Helen frowned. "Did he tell you that? That he just wanted to be friends?"

"Sure."

"Trish told me she thought he was going to ask her to prom that night."

Justin cocked his head. "Gavin never mentioned any plans to ask her."

"I know Trish had wanted to go out with him for a long time before they started dating," Helen said. "I'm not sure if it was love on her part or a big crush."

Sergio considered. "What about Allyson O'Brian?"

"Trish's little sister? What about her?"

"Did she have a crush on Gavin too?"

His eyes rolled in thought. "Could be. Most of the girls did since Gavin was a jock and all. But she wasn't there that night." Helen saw a flicker of understanding kick to life in his eyes. "Was she?"

Sergio didn't give anything away. "That's uncertain, but she was at the lodge Friday, even though she wasn't attending the cattlemen's convention. Do you know why she was there?"

He nodded. "Yeah, but it wasn't for any nefarious reason. She's looking for a dressage horse. She called me about it since I have contacts. I work for a feed supplier, but I pretty much know every horse person in the area. I arranged for her to meet with Tom Rourke. He's a broker, and I knew he had some horses that might suit her."

"I know Tom," Helen said. "He's a longtime friend of Chad's father."

"Are you and Allyson friends?" Sergio asked Justin.

"Acquaintances more like. I was surprised to hear from her. We had coffee a few times over the years but… it's awkward."

"How so?"

"She uh…well…kinda had a crush on me in high school, too, I think. That's what Trish said anyway. Nothing serious, just teen girl stuff. Trish said Allyson was like gum stuck to her shoe. They had a sibling rivalry thing going on. Far as I can tell, she wasn't ever a suspect in Trish's murder. I don't remember hearing anything about it. I mean, she was just a kid, fourteen I think."

"Old enough to commit murder," Sergio said slowly.

Justin flinched. "I never really thought of that before. But I don't think that's what happened. I mean, they're sisters. She couldn't have killed her own sister, could she? Even if she was jealous?"

"I'm sure not," Helen said, but doubt slithered through her stomach. Could Allyson actually have killed Trish?

"We have to go, Justin," Sergio said and Helen thanked him again for the flowers.

As they drove away from the ranch, Helen tumbled the thoughts through her mind. "I just can't believe that Allyson is a murderer."

"Maybe you and Justin are too sentimental toward people you knew back in your high school days."

She bridled. "Or maybe we have a clearer idea because we know the players and you don't."

"I think you're biased. If Allyson had motive enough to kill her sister, I'm going to treat her like a suspect."

His expression was granite, no hint of the earlier warmth.

"No stone unturned?" she said softly.

"Exactly."

After a call to Betty to update her on his whereabouts, Sergio drove to the highway. The road to Allyson O'Brian's home took them along the coast. Helen rolled down the window, inhaling the essence of salt in the air. The waters along the shore were rough and rocky, but the sound of the waves called to him. How long had it been since he enjoyed a free afternoon at the shore? Too long.

She gazed out along the shoreline, the breeze tugging at tendrils of her hair, freeing it from the ponytail. She pulled the elastic away, and the mass of auburn tumbled loose. With a sigh, she laid her head back against the seat.

"Tired?"

"A little," she admitted without opening her eyes. He stole sideways glances at her, noting the thick lashes and delicate cheekbones, hair caught between the copper color of fall leaves and the first rays of dawn. Helen, he could not deny, was a stunner. Not beauty-pageant gorgeous, but with a healthy down-to-earth quality that made it hard for him to keep from looking at her. She wore her sincerity on her sleeve and he found that quality irresistible.

Pay attention to the case, he told himself. "What were your impressions about Allyson?"

He regretted that his question made her open her eyes and sit straighter, but at least it edged away the fuzziness that got inside him when he looked at her.

"I'm embarrassed to say that I didn't take the time to get to know her. I was at Trish's house on and off, a very nice home on the bluff which they sold after the murder, but I never really paid much attention to Allyson."

"The family has money?"

She nodded. "They owned several properties, hotels, I believe throughout the state. Her dad traveled continually. They wanted their girls to have a small-town community to grow up in."

Look how that turned out. "Do you agree with Justin's assessment? That Trish and her sister didn't get along?"

"She made some comments, I recall. I do remember Trish asking to hang out at my house to escape her pesky sister, but, uh…" Helen looked uncertain. "We didn't have people over much, or ever, to be factual."

"Why not?"

"Again with the nosy questions."

"Guilty."

She let out a long, slow breath. "My mother was killed in a car accident for which my father was at fault, and after that he sort of abdicated. He desperately needed mental health treatment, but he refused to get it. We were little kids at the time, and Liam raised me, took care of things and prevented us from winding up in a foster home. Dad eventually developed a drinking problem when we were in high school, and he would disappear for weeks at a time, so we ran the household together, Liam more than me, but it was certainly not a *House Beau-*

tiful type of situation." A frown creased her brow. "He worked two jobs and I had one plus our school schedules, so there wasn't much time for socializing anyway." She blushed. "I… I didn't want anyone to know how we lived. We just sort of pretended our dad was still present and functioning. Liam handled everything from paying the bills to helping me with college applications when the time came."

"Your brother is quite a guy."

"Yes, he's my hero. I'm so glad he found Maggie. They're perfect for each other. God meant for them to be together, I'm sure of it."

He winced.

She cocked her head. "You don't go for that sort of thing?"

He sighed. "I want to. Fiona and I were raised to be faithful people. She was a better Christian."

She quirked a look at him. "There isn't a grading scale for Christians. We're all just a big family and no one's better than anyone else."

"I'm too angry to be in that family just now."

Her smile was gentle. "Believers are entitled to be angry."

"But they aren't supposed to want revenge and that's what I want." Out it came, the truth, in one unyielding lump. "I want someone to pay for Fiona's death, to answer for taking away Lucy and Laurel's mother. I want someone to pay for taking away my dreams and my career, as selfish as that sounds. I want it so bad it eclipses everything else in my life. I'm supposed to leave vengeance to the Lord, but I want it for me."

He saw the muscles work in her throat as she swallowed. "I guess I've gone another route. I neglected your sister, Sergio, and that contributed to her death, so I guess some of your need for vengeance should be directed toward me."

That made him pause. He would have probably agreed with her until he'd seen her with his girls, pulled her from the smothering pillow, witnessed the care and kindness she lavished on everyone. It startled him. How could he still want her to suffer after being privy to that? "I was wrong about that," he said quietly. "Wrong about dumping my feelings on you." He gripped the wheel, not daring to look at her. "Anyway, I don't want the girls to have a father who is tied up by anger, but I just can't let it go." He rubbed a hand over his chin. "They deserve a parent like they had in Fiona."

"They have a really good parent," she said, clasping his forearm. "One really amazing parent is all they need. You are a blessing in their lives."

A blessing? He tried to deflect the wave of emotion. "I couldn't even figure out how to potty train them. Betty finally tackled the issue by promising them Princess underwear or some such thing I never would have thought of."

"Lots of parents are stumped by that one."

Helen's touch made his body tingle. "That's only the tip of a very massive iceberg."

"You try your best and you get help when you need it. That's all any parent can do." She let her hand drift away and stared out the window. He wondered if she was thinking about her own father, and how different her life might have been if he had asked for help.

Her phone buzzed with a text. "Got a reprieve. Liam says there's a terrible storm delaying his return, so Aunt Ginny decided not to tell him quite yet what's going on here since he can't get home anyway. Otherwise, he's liable to commandeer an airplane and fly home, storm or no storm."

"Is he a pilot?"

"No. Retired Green Beret, but he'd convince someone to fly him. He's a force to be reckoned with."

"Well that's more incentive then, to get this case cracked open before Brother Beret returns." It made him feel better to say it, more in control of the strange pinwheeling emotions he felt sitting there next to her.

He slowed for a moment, gaze locked on the rear-view mirror.

She craned her neck. "What?"

"Thought I saw a vehicle behind us."

"Someone following us?"

He didn't answer for a minute. After an endless pause, he relaxed. "Nothing. Must have been mistaken."

She nodded and settled a little as if bracing herself for what was to come. It occurred to him that Trish's death was a cold case to law enforcement, a means to catch Fiona's killer to him, but it was so much more for Gavin, Justin, Helen and Trish's family. He felt a surge of guilt that he had not realized it sooner. Murder crashed through families like tidal waves, leaving wreckage spread far and wide.

But justice could mend some of that damage, couldn't it? If nothing else, he told himself, vengeance was preferable to helplessness any day of the week.

As he took the steep cliff trail to Allyson's family home, he thought that if the killer was responsible for both women's deaths, the vengeance would be all the sweeter.

NINE

The O'Brians' home was a lovely two-story structure that looked out on one side to a view of the rolling hills and the ocean beyond. White split-rail fences housed a pasture where two horses grazed in the late morning sun. They had purchased the residence after Trish's murder, probably since the old house would have been filled with remembrances of their lost child. Helen could not imagine how painful that must have been. Sometimes just looking at high school pictures of the five chums drove Helen to tears.

"Nice place," Sergio said as he parked the SUV at the end of the long driveway, bordered by neatly tended shrubbery.

Helen joined him in the long walk to the front step, and they rang the bell. Allyson opened the door. Helen's heart lurched at the face which resembled her long-gone sister's with some differences. Allyson's hair was cut into a pert pixie and dyed red. She was thinner than Trish, who had always bemoaned her curves. Helen remembered Trish trying out every weight-loss fad from the Grapefruit Diet to the fasting craze.

Helen introduced them. "Thank you for answering

my text and letting us stop by," she said. "This won't take long."

Allyson's blue eyes were curious and calm as she led them into a sitting room decorated in neutral tones except for a gorgeous Persian rug. A sleek Siamese cat twined around Helen's ankle.

"Sorry," Allyson said. "My parents are in Europe for a couple of weeks and the cat is needy." Her lip curled. "I'm not a cat person."

Helen bent to stroke the animal, receiving a rumbly purr for her troubles. "It's okay. I'm taking care of a dog who needs lots of affection too."

She waved them into a set of matching chairs and perched on the arm of the love seat across from them. "Chief Farraday told me what happened to you. That was pretty serious."

Helen nodded. "I'm okay," she said, before she realized that Allyson hadn't exactly asked about her well-being.

Allyson tucked a section of hair behind one ear. "I'm not sure what I can tell you that would help. I already explained to the chief why I was at the lodge. I'm in the market for a new dressage horse and Justin Dover gave me the name of a guy to talk to."

"Actually," Sergio said, "we're looking into a possible connection between your sister's murder and the death of Fiona Ross three years ago."

Allyson's gaze sharpened. "I didn't know they were related."

"That's what we're here to find out."

"Farraday didn't ask about anything like that."

Helen saw Sergio's mouth tighten. He was probably not the least bit surprised to know the chief hadn't pressed Allyson. "Do you have a theory about what happened to your sister?"

Helen sucked in a breath at Sergio's directness.

Allyson shrugged. "She was hit over the head with something and she died."

"Hit by whom?"

Allyson stared at him. "I don't know. Why would I? I wasn't even there."

"We thought she might have told you something, maybe about an enemy?"

Allyson broke into a hard, bitter guffaw. "Her biggest enemy was me. I couldn't stand my sister. I'm sorry if that shocks you, but she got way too many privileges, and everyone thought she was the cat's meow, especially the boys."

"You resented that?"

"Of course I did," Allyson spat. "Gavin, Justin and plenty of other guys flocked to her because she pretended to be fun and charming and whatever. It didn't hurt that our family had money either. Well I knew her, really knew her, and I can tell you she was petty and mean." She held up a palm. "Oh, I wouldn't wish her dead, and I didn't have anything to do with the murder. But people sometimes get what's coming to them in life, don't they?"

Helen hoped her expression wasn't revealing the revulsion she felt on the inside. Trish had been a genuine, selfless friend to Helen. She could not reconcile her perception with the picture Allyson was painting.

Allyson strode to the side table and snagged a hard candy from a cut-crystal bowl. "Look, I know how that makes me sound, but it's the truth. There's something to be said for honesty, right?"

Helen didn't know how to respond.

Sergio cut in. "Did you know my sister Fiona?"

Allyson looked at him hard. "Fiona was your sister?"

"Yes."

Allyson pursed her lips. "Oh, right. I see the resemblance now. I didn't know her well. I met her a few times when Trish entertained at the house, but after Trish died, that was that. We packed up and moved and tried to get on with our lives. I was surprised when Fiona came to see me."

Helen gaped, but again Sergio beat her to the question. "What? She came here? When?"

Allyson rolled the candy around her mouth. "Must have been three years ago now. At first I thought it was some sort of weird reunion or something, because I'd seen Gavin and Justin back in town at the horse competition. Odd that all of us were around at the same time, but small towns and horse competitions bring people together, I guess. Gavin was there with a girl on his arm, not much to look at. He married her, come to find out. Justin was his usual oblivious self unless he was making a sale."

Sergio was on the edge of his seat now. "Do you remember the exact date Fiona came to see you?"

"January eleventh. It stuck in my mind because I'd done well in the dressage competition that day and I was super stoked. I didn't really want to talk to her, but my parents pressured me. Take some time to see your sister's good friend, they said." Allyson rolled her eyes. "Fiona wasn't my friend ever and I didn't see the need to chat, but, you know, family obligation and all that."

Helen felt as though she could not breathe. January eleventh was the day before Fiona died. "What…what did she want to talk to you about, Allyson?"

"Nothing much. It was kind of strange. She made small talk, and then she asked me stuff about the past."

"What did she ask you specifically?" Sergio pressed.

Allyson shrugged. "I don't remember."

"It's really important," Helen said. "Can you remember anything from your conversation?"

Allyson tossed her head, sending her gold bracelets jangling. "I said I don't remember. Look, not to be rude, but I have to get going now." She walked them across the tile foyer and opened the front door.

"Did the police talk to you about Fiona's visit?" Sergio said.

"No."

"And you didn't contact them after you'd heard she'd been murdered?" Helen couldn't stop herself from asking the question.

Allyson shrugged. "I didn't see any point. I don't have any idea who might have killed her."

Sergio yanked a business card from his wallet and handed it over. "My cell number is on there. If you think of anything, remember any details, please call."

"Okay." They'd almost cleared the tiled porch when Allyson stopped them with a comment. "You know, she did ask me about a memory book, come to think of it."

Helen almost jumped. She gasped in astonishment. "The memory books. Fiona made them after the funeral, three of them. One for herself, one for me and one for you. They were filled with photos of some high school memories, dances and such, and pictures from the funeral. I completely forgot."

"Yeah, anyway, she wanted to see mine, but I told her I didn't have it anymore."

"Where is it?" Sergio asked.

"I threw it away." She leveled a cold glance at Sergio. "Don't give me that look, okay? Maybe you were really close to your sister and that's nice and all, but I wasn't. What's done is done. Her murder will probably always be unsolved and frankly, I don't really care what happened that night. I've made peace with it and moved on."

Helen looked away in disbelief. Could Trish's death really have meant so little to her sister? In a fog, she thanked Allyson and followed Sergio back to the car.

The fact kept reverberating through her brain like a loudly struck gong.

Fiona had been to see Allyson the day before her death.

The stark lines that cut around Sergio's mouth told her he was thinking the same thing.

They hadn't made it to the edge of the property, before he rounded on her.

"Your memory book. Where is it?"

"I was just mulling that over. Gus and Ginny let me store some belongings in the lodge basement, since there's very little space in my room. There are some boxes."

"Could it be there?"

"Maybe, but I honestly don't remember what I still own from high school. I moved a few times after Liam went into the service before I landed the job at the lodge. Are you thinking Fiona was looking for the book?"

"It fits with the note she left for herself."

Trish. Proof.
Find out who still has theirs.

As in…who still had their memory book?

They hurried to the car. Helen was just buckling up

when she sat bolt upright in her seat as if an electric current had passed through her.

Sergio shot her a look. “You remember something.”

She nodded. “Fiona mentioned that she’d brought her memory book with her when she came up for the weekend. We were going to look through it, but…” She gulped. “Well, you know what happened. I’d told her I didn’t know where mine was anymore, so that’s probably why she went to Allyson.”

He guided the SUV along, eyes shifting in thought. “Fiona found something in her memory book that implicated someone for Trish’s murder. But why would she ask Allyson if she still had hers if Fiona’d gotten her own proof?”

“I think I know the answer to that question.” Helen struggled to peel back the years to get to the memory. “Fiona said her book was water damaged, from a flooded storage room.”

Sergio thumped his hand on the steering wheel. “That’s right. I remember a phone call we had. Soon after her marriage, before the twins came along, they’d had a burst pipe in their apartment. Some stuff got ruined. Her book must have sustained some damage so she was looking for another copy of whatever photo caught her attention.” He took a turn slowly as the road began to dip steeply down. “The killer knows what Fiona was looking for, that’s why she was run down. That’s the reason someone set fire to the cabin and searched your room. They’re looking for the memory book. Who knew about the books?”

“Fiona gave them to us at a memorial a few weeks after the funeral, so anyone who was there might have seen us with them.”

"Gavin, Justin, Allyson."

"The whole town, practically. Plus Chief Farraday and Trish's family, of course."

"Of course."

Helen's blood ran cold at the way he said it, prickling her skin in goose bumps.

"Do you recall if there were any photos of Allyson in that book?"

She thought hard. "I just don't remember. I'm sorry."

"I think we better lay our hands on your copy as soon as possible."

"What if it's not there in the basement?"

Sergio's mouth thinned into a grim line. "There's only one way to find out."

Helen jumped as her phone buzzed with a quick succession of texts. "Uh-oh. Chad and Mitch are not happy to find that I've fled the coop. I'll update them and explain we're on our way to the lodge. They can meet us there and help look."

She tapped a long message into her phone, imagining her brothers' frustration that she'd not told them beforehand of their trip. "I don't like to worry them."

He sighed. "You know, I should probably be annoyed at their attitude, but the fact is I wish I'd have been more like that to Fiona. I'd give anything to have the chance to be a big brother again."

Helen reached out to touch his shoulder when his body went wire taut.

"Helen…"

"What is it?"

The car began to accelerate.

"Slow down, Sergio," she said.

"I can't. We have no brakes."

Inch by inch the SUV picked up speed. The black rocks of the cliffside streaked by as the car shimmied closer and closer to the edge of control.

She clung to the door handle and prayed.

TEN

Sergio downshifted, but the vehicle accelerated anyhow. As the rocks flashed by on either side of the car, he fought to keep to his side of the road. Their speed increased. He pumped the brakes frantically with no response.

Helen was still and silent next to him, but he could hear her quickened breaths.

"Jump out, Helen, before we're moving any faster. I'll stay to try and make sure I don't hit anyone else that might be coming up."

"No."

"Helen," he said more firmly this time. "It just gets worse from here. You've got to jump."

"I'm not leaving you."

"Listen…"

"Stop it, Sergio." Her words snapped out like the crackle of electricity. "I'm not leaving you, not like I did to Fiona."

He groaned. "This isn't about Fiona." He'd thought everything between them was about Fiona, but now all he could hold on to was getting Helen safely out before the inevitable crash. In that moment everything vanished but the need to keep her safe.

The fender slammed into a finger of rock that was grating against the metal. She cried out but did not allow a full-fledged scream. He fought the wheel as they skidded by. Once more he tried to command her to save herself, but now she would not even look at him.

Plan B. He had to come up with something. "I'm going to find a place to pull the parking brake, hope it will force us to skid out."

"Where? This road is nothing but twists and turns."

"I remember about halfway down there was one spot that might work." One spot, one chance. If it didn't… No. He would make sure Helen survived, plus he had two daughters to go home to, didn't he? *Come on, God. If you're listening right now, help me, would You?* So many lives hung in the balance.

His fingers cramped from gripping the steering wheel. "I'll tell you when, okay?"

She nodded, scared but in control…a brave woman. Her lips moved, and he knew she was praying. They careened down the cliffside, taking the turns so fast he thought he could feel the wheels leave the pavement. Again the car bumped against the rocks, the metal screaming in protest.

He rounded the next turn. *Please don't let anyone else be coming up*, he found himself saying. They were getting close to the point where he would not be able to keep the car from plunging off the road, tumbling down to the ocean or hitting the rock wall at full speed.

Ahead the lane widened into a shallow turnout. It wasn't much, barely enough room for a large truck, but it was their best chance.

"Ready?"

"Ready," she said, voice shaky.

As they drew alongside the turnout, he jammed on the parking break. The SUV shuddered in protest, skidding sideways. He turned into the skid. They slid off the road, toward the craggy wall. Though his brain knew it was no use, he practically stood on the brakes. Two feet, then three, a matter of seconds and the SUV plowed into the rock.

The impact caused them both to pitch forward. With a sharp bang, the airbags deployed at the same time. He heard Helen scream, and then her cry was lost against the billow of white.

With the impact still ringing in his ears, he racked his seat back, freeing himself from the slowly deflating airbag. He staggered around to the passenger door and opened it with shaking fingers.

Helen did not look at him, chin bowed to her chest.

"Hey," he reached for her forearm, a sensation of terror running through him that he'd only felt twice before. The first happened when he'd been in the shoe store helping Lucy try on a pair of school shoes and he'd looked around to discover that Laurel had wandered off. He'd been shouting and ready to call the National Guard, SWAT and the Navy SEALs just as the clerk returned Laurel to him from behind a stack of boxed rain boots. The second, when he'd pulled Helen's head from the pillow. "Helen?" he forced out, silently pleading.

She raised her head then, pale and panting, and fired a wan smile at him. "At least we know the airbags work," she said shakily.

He couldn't speak for a moment. "Are you hurt?"

She took mental stock and then shook her head. "I don't think so. How about you?"

"No. Let me help you." As tenderly as he could, he assisted her from the car and into his arms.

"Wait," she said, bending back toward the car and retrieving Laurel's bunny. "You're going to need a tow and we can't let this little guy get lost."

Always the practical woman. The car's front end was crumpled, the windshield shattered. She was shaking, and he was a tad unsteady himself as he led her from the car and held her close, relishing the tickle of her hair on his cheek, her softness against his chest.

He moved her as far away from the road as he could and helped her sit on a rock while he dialed the police who promised to dispatch a unit and an ambulance, which Helen might just be stubborn enough to decline. He would put off that battle for a short while. His second call went to Chad. To his credit, Chad took the news with a steadiness that might have come from working with two-thousand-pound animals who could crush a man with one unpredictable move.

"I'm on my way," he said, through what sounded like gritted teeth.

He checked on Helen again, looking for signs of shock. She was a bit dazed, perhaps, but alert. He took off his jacket and draped it over her shoulders before he edged around the wrecked SUV. Sliding onto his back, he squirmed under, ignoring the pain in his bruised shoulders from the airbag deployment. It took him only a moment before he crawled out again and stood, lost in thought.

"What is it?" Helen cradled the bunny. He considered not telling her, but she'd stayed with him, refusing to save herself and it would not do her justice to hide the truth from her.

"Someone sliced the brake line," he said.

Her eyes opened wide. "While we were talking to Allyson?"

"Yeah, so who knew we were coming here? Allyson, Justin, Gavin."

"And Farraday, but I guess he doesn't count."

"He counts. He's a cop who doesn't want us to look into Trish's death."

She groaned. "So they could all know, but why would any of them try to kill us?"

"I can think of only one reason. To keep us from finding that memory book."

Helen grimaced. He thought she might cry, but instead she put her head up and fired him a look of steely green-eyed determination. "Then we'd better make sure we find it first."

He could not resist kissing her forehead. "Yes, ma'am, we will."

Chad and Mitch arrived at the same time as the ambulance.

"I'm not going to the hospital," Helen announced. "I just got out of that place."

"All the more reason to go back," Mitch said. Because her head was aching, and she was outnumbered three to one, she gave in. "Fine, but Sergio's going to have to go too and get checked out or I'm not going either."

Sergio opened his mouth to protest and then closed it after the matching glares he received from both brothers. "Fair enough."

"I'll alert Aunt Ginny and Uncle Gus, then head over and start searching the basement for that photo book," Chad said.

Mitch nodded. “I’ll stay with these two.”

Helen sighed. “Do you get the feeling we’re being managed like a couple of kids?”

Sergio nodded. “Now I know how Laurel and Lucy feel.” He snuck a look at his cell phone, while the paramedics checked his vitals. “Betty has to get a tooth fixed today so I have to be there for the girls at 1:00 p.m. She’s already rescheduled it twice. Maybe I should…”

“You’re going to the hospital,” Helen said firmly. “We’ll probably be free by 1:00 p.m. and if we aren’t, I will ask Aunt Ginny to stay with the girls.”

Sergio opened his mouth to reply, but Mitch shook his head. “Trust me. On this one, you lose.”

“All right. I concede.” Sergio went quiet. “Mitch, you’re a law enforcement type.”

“Former.”

“No such thing as a former US marshal, if I’m correct.”

Another slight smile indicated Mitch’s approval. “What’s on your mind?”

“Farraday. Odd that he’s so reluctant to look into Trish’s death. He didn’t even ask Allyson about a possible connection, and apparently he didn’t look closely at her as a suspect all those years ago. Plus that thing with the shooter, Kyle Burnette. I couldn’t find anything much on him. Petty stuff, misdemeanors.”

“I’ll work on it. Dig deeper.”

With all that had happened, she’d almost forgotten about the man who’d taken a shot at them near the tunnels. *Just breathe*, she told herself. *One thing at a time.*

As she’d expected, the doctors concluded there was nothing seriously wrong with either one of them, save for bumps and bruises from the airbag and the impact.

They'd been released shortly after noon, just after Chad reported he'd found no trace of the memory book in the basement and they'd dutifully reported every last detail of the crash to an officer from the Driftwood Police Department.

Against Chad's protests, Helen promised to come help him as soon as she could. She and Sergio headed down in the elevator, passing through the lobby where she stopped at the sight of a curly haired pregnant woman staring at her cell phone, Gavin's wife.

"Dee?" Helen said.

The woman looked up. "Yes?"

"I'm Helen Pike. I manage the Roughwater Lodge where you're staying. Your husband and I went to high school together."

"Oh. So you're the Helen that…" She pushed her hair from her face. "Um, I mean you were there when the tragedy happened in those tunnels all those years ago."

"Yes."

Her slight smile vanished. "And my husband says you're digging into it again."

"Investigating a few things."

"Well, stop, won't you please?" Her expression was pleading with a streak of anger mixed in. "He's been hurt enough by what happened. You all have. What can be gained from raking it all up again?"

"Justice," Sergio said. "No one ever paid for Trish's death."

"What good is that now? It was fifteen years ago. Everyone has moved on. Why can't you do the same?"

Helen started to reply that Trish's parents would likely never be able to move on, when Gavin stepped through the front entrance. His mouth opened in surprise and he hastened over. "Hey." He dropped a kiss on his wife's cheek. "I'm sorry I'm late." He looked at Helen and Sergio. "We're here for an ultrasound. Routine, everything is normal," he hastened to add, draping an arm around his wife.

"The doctor is running late," Dee said.

"Then I'm not in trouble," Gavin added.

Helen glimpsed the same charming smile that snagged Gavin the lead role in the school musical three years running. Back then he'd split his time between theater, basketball and the cross-country track team. "I was out for a walk in the woods behind the lodge and the time got away from me." He looked at Helen. "What are you two doing here?"

Their reply was interrupted when a nurse poked her head from behind a door. "Mr. and Mrs. Cutter? The doctor is ready for you now."

"What do you make of her reaction?" Sergio inquired as they headed out and climbed into the extra ranch truck Mitch had brought over.

"It makes sense, I guess. Dee knows how the past injured Gavin and she doesn't want it all dragged up again. I might feel the same way if I was in her shoes."

"Nah, you've got too much grit for that," Sergio said.

She blushed, oddly pleased at the compliment.

"Why wouldn't she want his name cleared once and for all?" He paused. "Unless she knows he wasn't as innocent as he professes to be."

Helen's head spun with too many theories, her body aching from their crash. Opening the window, she let the wind rush in to sweep the cobwebs from her mind, but nothing became clearer as they arrived at the lodge grounds. The time was tight, almost one o'clock, so she went with Sergio to the cabin.

They met Betty in the yard. Lucy and Laurel were busily examining a rain-filled puddle.

Betty raised an eyebrow. "Where's your SUV?"

"Long story. Point is I made it in time."

Though she looked at him curiously, she did not question him further. Both girls finally looked up from their puddle perusal and beelined over to Sergio. He caught them up and twirled them around, though it cost him a wince of pain as he settled them back to earth again. Betty had dressed them in matching blue overalls and done their hair in pigtails. They looked so small in their denim outfits, so full of joy at seeing Sergio again.

Adorable, Helen thought, with that peculiar swirl of sadness and pleasure.

"I'll just go help Chad," she said.

"We're fishin'," Laurel said, eyes sparkling. "Wanna fish?"

"Stay." Sergio held on to her forearm. "Like she said, we're fishin'."

Lucy offered her a stick, her face so serious Helen had to smother a laugh.

Sergio wiggled his brows. "How can you resist an offer like that?"

"I suspect you don't want me to go off searching without you."

Sergio feigned innocence. "Me? Where would you get an idea like that?" There was a gleam of emotion in his brown eyes she could not identify, a lingering warmth where his palm touched her shoulder.

"I would just feel better if I could keep you in my sights," he admitted, when she fixed him with a look. "It will only be a little while before Betty gets back." The tone was light, but it tickled her nerves. It's the case, she told herself. He wants to be there for every moment, to avenge his sister, not for any other reason. Yet the flutter in her stomach remained. Armed with her stick, she took Lucy's small hand and marched over to the puddle.

Chad would alert her with a text if he found anything at all. Evonne, Tiny and the staff had everything handled at the lodge. For now, perhaps the best use of her time was to be with the girls, even though Sergio desired her proximity for ulterior motives.

She'd stay for a while, spend time with the girls, allow her nerves to settle from the most recent threat to her safety. It hurt to be near them, though, a reminder of the cost of her long-ago choice. If she'd only taken time to meet with Fiona on that fateful day, perhaps the situation would be completely different.

The girls would have their mother.

Sergio would still be a brother.

And Helen would not feel the steady beat of guilt in her soul. Walking with the two motherless girls cleaved her heart.

Show me how to live with this, Father.

Or show me how to let it go.

ELEVEN

By the time they'd finished their fishing expedition, both girls were coated in mud. He marched them straightaway to the bathtub, adding a hefty squirt of bubble juice, as they called it. He'd convinced Helen to stay, but he realized she would not be content to linger there much longer. He didn't quite understand his own level of desperation at the thought of her leaving. It was ridiculous. Her brother Chad was right there in the lodge and the place was chock-full of people. She was safe, perfectly safe, yet he could not stomach the notion of her being away from him. Why?

His fear made no sense, until he explained it away. He desired to protect his sister's best friend, no doubt, loyalty to the person Fiona had loved. That was it. But when she'd sat there in the ruined car, chin down, not answering him, it had not felt like simple loyalty.

Lucy got shampoo in her eyes and began to wail. While he lifted her from the tub and comforted her, Laurel bonked her chin on the faucet and began to cry too. The sobbing echoed in the small room as he tried to simultaneously dry off Lucy and comfort Laurel.

Helen appeared at his elbow holding a fluffy towel. "Need a hand?"

Gratefully he bundled Lucy into her arms and lifted Laurel from the cooling water. When she was tolerably dry, he rooted through the suitcase for what he hoped passed for a decent outfit, pink sweatpants and a long-sleeved shirt to suit the cold weather.

Laurel shook her head. "I want the pony top."

This was a new development. Formerly she'd not really cared how he'd dressed her. He stood there paralyzed with indecision. He'd read that choices were important for young girls, but conversely it wasn't a good idea to allow them to undermine parental authority. He tried to think how his mother might have handled it, but he honestly could not recall one time he'd cared about what he wore as a kid and he had no clue how she'd dealt with his sister. His mind accelerated into the future. What was going to happen when they became teenagers and wanted to have boyfriends? His throat clogged. And when they started to drive? Visions of teenage catastrophe swirled as he stood like a statue with the shirt in his hands.

Helen popped her head in. "Lucy picked out her unicorn shirt to wear. It looked too thin for the weather since she wants to go outside again, so I added a sweatshirt."

"Ah. Great. No problem. Perfect." He gave Laurel the pony top and slid the long-sleeved shirt over it. Problem solved. Why hadn't he thought of that?

Betty returned just as Helen was leaving. He helped Betty settle them at the kitchen table with coloring books and ran to catch up with Helen. The lodge was bustling as usual and she stopped briefly to wipe up a tiny drip at the coffee station and talk to Evonne.

"Everything's going great," Evonne said. "Don't worry."

"I wasn't a bit worried," she said with a squeeze of

Evonne's hand. They headed along a hallway and pushed through the doors that led down into the basement where they found Chad kneeling next to a pile of boxes.

He offered a wry smile. "So far I've found your spelling bee medal from fourth grade, a box of teddy bears and a bunch of old concert ticket stubs, but the rest of this stuff seems to be related to lodge business."

Helen moved closer to peer at the labels written in Sharpie on the cardboard. "We replaced the dishware and linens last year. These are all the old ones."

Chad shot her a grin, wriggling a stuffed animal. "I didn't know you had such a thing for teddy bears. They're all dressed in pink."

She sighed. "I had a thing for pink too." She reached for the toy and cradled a fuzzy bear to her cheek. "Daddy gave me this one on my sixth birthday."

Warmth circled inside Sergio. She'd had to put away her childhood early after her mother's accident. Maybe that's why it meant so much to her to take care of people, her guests, her brothers, the girls. She had so much love to give, he thought.

Chad regarded her with a quickly concealed flash of pain. "Yeah. Guess I have some things from happier days too."

Sergio didn't know Chad's story, but he'd learned a few facts. Chad's father captained a charter boat which sank, resulting in fatalities. He'd been jailed for manslaughter due to his blood alcohol level. What kind of effect did that have on a son? Chad busied himself retaping the opened boxes.

Sergio refocused. "Which ones haven't you looked through?"

Chad pointed out the untouched cartons. They

searched every remaining one with no further success. The memory book was simply not there. His tension grew with each passing minute. First the attack on Helen, then his car. The clock was ticking.

Helen sighed and sank down on a card chair. "This is getting us nowhere, and I'm starved. Let's go get something from the kitchen."

"Which will give you an opportunity to check on Tiny?" Chad said.

Her cheeks pinked. "I'm sure he's doing fine, but yes, it wouldn't hurt to see if he needs anything. I recalculated the purchase invoice to account for the seven vegetarian diners, but I want to be sure I figured correctly."

Chad checked his phone. "Mitch is coming. He's got something to tell us."

Helen put the bear back into a box and carefully closed up the cardboard flaps. "I hope his time has been more fruitful than ours."

Sergio eyed her carefully. She looked beyond tired and he wanted to suggest that she lie down for a while, but he knew she would reject the idea.

They gave the basement one last glance before they shut the lights out and headed for the kitchen. Another dead end and not one step closer to any kind of an answer.

A wall of enticing aroma hit them as they entered the kitchen. Tiny was singing away, sliding pans of cookies out of the oven. Sergio's mouth watered at the aroma wafting from the golden cookies studded with glossy chocolate chips. Waving off any assistance, Helen dished them up bowls of leftover chili and a plate of warm cookies, with an extra serving for Mitch, and carried them on a tray to a small seating area on the lodge grounds. From there, Sergio could see all the way to the cabin where his girls were hopefully napping with the watchful Betty on duty. It eased his mind. That, and the fact that he'd locked all the windows and attached portable alarms to the front and back doors. There would be no way anyone could enter the house without Sergio or Betty knowing. It was probably overkill, since there were no direct threats to the girls, but it reassured him anyway.

The low stone wall offered them a respite from the wind and some privacy, though they were still within sight of the guests who strolled the grounds, some heading for the corral to enjoy a late afternoon ride.

Jingles raced over to Helen, bumping her knee in the process. She cooed and massaged his ears. "Missed me, huh?"

"Yeah." Mitch crammed his big frame into a chair and dug into his bowl of chili. "He's tunneled under the fence twice to bust out and come back here so I figured we'd save some work and bring him along."

Though Jingles had proven to be an ineffectual guard dog, Sergio was glad to have him around simply because he encouraged Helen's effervescent smile.

"Got intel on the second cop who investigated Trish O'Brian's murder," Mitch said. "Frank Higgins. Interestingly, he didn't last long as a cop. Quit six months after Trish's death."

Sergio frowned, instincts prickling. "Really?"

"Really. He works for a rental car company and coincidentally, he's traveling through the area on his return from a business trip tomorrow morning. He said he'd come by the ranch for a chat." Mitch wiped his mouth. "Didn't want to talk on the phone."

Sergio put down the cookie he'd been about to eat. "You think he's got something to help us?"

"Time will tell." Mitch looked at Chad. "You or me tonight?"

Chad spooned up his last bite of chili. "Me. You've got the farrier first thing tomorrow."

Mitch nodded.

Helen huffed. "Why do I get the feeling there's a plan afoot?"

Neither brother looked at her. "We're gonna take turns sleeping in your parlor on the sofa," Mitch said in the direction of his empty bowl.

Helen put her spoon down with a clank. "No, you're not. I'm fine. I had the lock changed and Sergio had a camera installed at the top of the stairs."

"Not good enough," Mitch said and Chad bobbed his head in agreement.

"It most certainly is good enough," she snapped.

Mitch leveled a look at Sergio. "What's your vote, you being more impartial than her brothers?"

Sergio shook his head. "Sorry, Helen, but it's the safest thing."

She groaned, snagged a cookie from the platter and chomped off a bite. "I'm being bullied."

"Not bullied, loved," Chad said. "Assertively."

Sergio was about to try and smooth things over, when his attention was riveted over Mitch's shoulder. He had to be mistaken. He stood, to get a better look at the short man strolling past the front of the lodge, in the direction of the side entrance. Thick waist, curly hair, wearing his nonchalance like a badge.

Mitch and Chad were on their feet now too, the question plain on their faces.

"I just saw Kyle Burnette."

He didn't have to say it twice. The two brothers fell in behind him as they raced to intercept.

It took Helen and Jingles a moment to understand what was going on. Jingles ping-ponged his attention between the running men and Helen, until she and the dog both took off after them. Passing the graveled drive and skirting the grass, they came into view of the side door. She saw Burnette step up close behind a guest as he used his key card to access the entrance. Not just a guest, Justin Dover, who was chatting with a rancher. Burnette intended to slip into the lodge just behind him. Sergio outpaced Mitch and Chad. As he closed the gap, Burnette jerked a look behind him and spotted his pursuers. He pivoted and ran toward the woods behind the property.

Jingles, finally figuring out the object of their quarry, flew at Burnette, quickly covering the distance between them until he was even with Sergio.

Go, Jingles.

Sergio reached out a hand, fingertips inches from Burnette's jacket, when he stumbled over an uneven patch of ground, skidding headfirst onto the grass and tumbling over and over. Burnette sprinted away toward the woods, Jingles still hot on his heels.

"I'll get a horse," Chad shouted. "See if I can track him in the woods."

"I'll go on foot," Mitch hollered and they headed in different directions. Helen hurried to Sergio who was picking himself up, muttering.

"Are you okay?"

"Yeah, I'm fine. Just mad at myself. I could have had him."

"You were close, for sure." She brushed at some twigs caught in his hair, her fingers skimming his cheek. He caught her palm, brought it closer, his breath warming her skin. He held her there, the connection between them easy and gentle. Her pulse pattered in a way that made her forget Sergio was Fiona's brother, forced her heart to acknowledge that the feelings she had for him were changing. He'd started out as a reminder of all the ways she'd failed, but now...

Justin was hurrying toward them. She detached herself, looked away. Sergio seemed relieved as well, still catching his breath, brushing off the dirt from his jeans and jacket.

"I happened to look back and saw you all in a panic. What's going on?"

"Thought we saw a stranger trying to sneak into the lodge is all," Sergio panted.

"Who?"

"Short guy, curly hair, trespassing," he puffed. "No problem. He's gone."

Justin's gaze was troubled. "Is this guy responsible for the earlier attack in your room, Helen?"

She resisted a shiver. "I don't know. Please, go catch up to your colleagues. I don't want you to miss the presentation."

Reluctantly, Justin walked back into the lodge.

They stayed there, watching to see if Burnette would circle back in their direction, but he didn't. Mitch returned a half hour later with Jingles panting alongside him, and texted Chad to return. "He had a vehicle. He's gone."

Helen felt like screaming. "What did he want here? The memory book? But how would he have found out about it?"

"Allyson? Farraday? Gavin and Justin?" Sergio's tone was bitter. "Any of them or none of them."

Mitch was thoughtful. “Burnette wanted to keep you away from the tunnels. His police file says he was interviewed by the cops a couple of times over the years. Rumored to have been transporting illegal drugs before the Driftwood PD shut down that operation.”

Helen tried to make sense of it. “They haven’t started up again, have they? Was Burnette hired by his people to keep us out?”

“I talked to Danny Patron,” Mitch said with a look at Sergio. “The current police chief. He’s out on leave.”

“I know him a little. He handled the murder investigation for my sister.”

“Kept things short, since Danny has to focus on his daughter’s recovery, but he said he doesn’t think they’ve started moving product again. Says he would have known about it.”

“So if it’s not to protect some drug interests, why is Burnette so keen on keeping us out of those tunnels?” Helen mused aloud.

“And why does he want to sneak into the lodge? Maybe he tracked us to Allyson’s and tampered with the brakes on my SUV, hoping that would take us out of the equation permanently.”

Permanently. Helen thought about how close Burnette had been to slipping into the lodge unnoticed. From there, there were a good many places he could have hidden until dark, when he could enact whatever plan he’d embarked on.

She felt again the numbing helplessness at being drugged and slowly smothered, brought back from the brink of death only because Sergio had found her. She shivered, and Sergio took her hand and pressed a kiss to her knuckle. He looked at Mitch. “I’m going to install a camera just outside the guest entrance, unless you have an objection."

"No objection from me," Mitch said.

Sergio kept hold of her hand, which had gone cold. "I'll keep watch from the cabin. He won't get near the place again."

Maybe it wasn't such a bad thing to have one of her brothers sleeping on the sofa, and Sergio Ross watching from his cabin on the other side of the property. She wished just for a second, that Sergio would wrap her in his arms and help her push the fear away.

Silly thought. He's here to solve a case, she told herself.

That's all.

And he was your best friend's brother.

Sergio's brow furrowed.

"What is it?" she said. "You've just thought of something else, haven't you?"

"I'm naturally suspicious."

"Suspicions keep you alive in the law enforcement business," Mitch said. "Spill it."

"It occurred to me that maybe Burnette arranged with Justin to follow him into the lodge."

Helen gaped. "Why would he do that?"

"I don't know," Sergio said, "but like Mitch says, it pays to be suspicious."

Suspicious? Helen's thoughts rolled in every direction. At what point did suspicious turn into paranoia? How could she do her job while scanning the multitudes of guests, wondering which had tried to kill her? Kill them both?

What dark place had she pried open when she'd found that letter of Fiona's?

Shivering, she hurried inside.

TWELVE

Helen tapped on Sergio's door the next morning at eight thirty. He answered, confused by her chuckle until he realized he was wearing an apron of Aunt Ginny's loaned to Betty for baking with the girls. It was a colorful cherry print, cinched around his middle.

His face went hot. "Oh, I was gonna try to make pancakes, but I didn't want to get it all over my jeans."

She allowed another giggle. "Quite all right. You look very fetching in an apron." She handed him a foil-wrapped plate. "Muffins left over after the chapel service. I thought the girls might enjoy them."

"You're a peach," he said, drawing her in.

"Again with your affinity for fruit. Girls still asleep?"

"Yes, but they're beginning to stir so I figured I'd help out on the breakfast front."

"Good daddy."

"Nah. Betty's the champ, but I try to do as much as I can."

She regarded him, eyes the color of new spring leaves. "They're blessed to have you for a father."

Blessed? That word again? He'd never figured it that way. "I should have been their uncle, not their father."

Absently, she straightened the napkins in their wicker holder. "I lost my mother and my father in different ways, but I have a brother who parents me, and Aunt Ginny and Uncle Gus, who aren't related, and Mitch and Chad. I guess I've learned that the love is more important than the title."

He was struck by the sincerity of it, the deep wisdom and peace from a woman so young, so tested by life. "I wasn't sure what they should call me, at first," he found himself saying. "I wasn't their father, but they didn't seem to want to call me Uncle Sergio anymore. All their playmates had daddies." He said it before he could stop himself. "The day Laurel called me Daddy I cried. I'm not sure it was out of happiness or fear or a combination of the two, but I'll never forget that day. Sometimes I feel like I stole the title without earning it, without…" He groped for words. "…deserving it," he finished.

"Like I said, the love is more important than the title." He froze as she came closer, smelling of coffee and shampoo. "But if it means anything, I think God appointed just the right person to be their father."

"And their godmother," he heard himself say.

She jerked, blinked, and in a moment the green eyes were glazed with tears. "I didn't know you knew that. I wanted to be there…but you…"

Now it was his turn to close the distance between them, taking her hand with a gentle squeeze. "I cut you out. You called and sent cards and I was a jerk and kept you out of their lives. That was wrong and I'm sorry."

She stared at their joined hands. "I understand. No matter how we sugarcoat it, my actions contributed to their mother's death. Maybe I'm the one that doesn't deserve their title."

He mourned the time he'd spent despising her, all the comments he'd made to shovel his own pain on top of hers. "I don't blame you anymore, Helen—I never should have in the first place." He leaned toward her and kissed her temple. "Maybe it's time for you to forgive yourself."

She stayed still for a moment and he heard her little gulp, the quick inhalation of breath before she stepped away. "I… I'll think about it. We should go. I know you probably want to be there when we speak to Frank Higgins at the ranch house."

His words were too much, too soon maybe, and she could not accept it. He nodded. "Absolutely. I'll drive you over, unless Chad's on duty."

"He's waiting outside with Jingles. I'll tell him you'll drive us…" she said over her shoulder, her mischievous smile in place, "…as soon as you change out of your adorable apron."

He sighed. In the past, he'd have taken that kind of teasing badly, an insult to his manhood. Since the girls came along, his macho persona had sunk down on the list of priorities. Besides, he felt only amusement from Helen, not judgement.

She was generous, thoughtful, meticulous about her business and passionate to help those she loved. He felt a peculiar squeeze in his chest that he'd been part of her pain. But here she was helping him realize he was deserving of the role of daddy. Perhaps, before he left Roughwater, he could encourage Helen to be a godmother to the girls, show her she deserved that title. Yes, he thought. Lucy and Laurel needed their godmother, which no doubt explained his ongoing preoccupation with Helen. Maybe God brought him here partly to accomplish that mission, along with solving

Fiona's murder. It was startling to think that God might be diverting him from his vengeance. He rejected the idea.

No offense, God, but that's still number one on my list.

Scarfing down a quick bite of muffin, he drove them to the Roughwater Ranch, Chad trailing along behind him. When they arrived, the family was already seated at the dining room table with a twitchy, sandy-haired man whose jeans and button-up shirt hung loose on his skinny frame. Chad strolled in behind them and Jingles scurried around to accept greetings from the assembled group.

"Frank Higgins," the stranger said, offering handshakes all around.

Aunt Ginny slid mugs of coffee in front of Sergio, Helen and Chad. "To catch you two up, Mr. Higgins said he was a new officer on the force fifteen years ago. He worked with Chief Farraday."

"He was my supervising sergeant then." Higgins dragged a thumb along his pointed chin. "I understand you're investigating the Trish O'Brian murder. May I ask why you aren't directing these questions to Farraday?"

"Because he's giving us the runaround," Sergio said flatly.

Higgins was silent for a moment. "I'm not surprised. I figured that someday there might be questions asked." He shook his head. "I should have spoken up at the time, but I was a rookie." He shrugged. "I didn't want to get fired."

Sergio's nerves jumped. "Spoken up about what exactly?"

Higgins surveyed them, punctuating each of his points by tapping a thick finger on the table. "First let me make it clear that I will not provide an official statement. This is all off-the-record. If it comes down to a formal interview, my memory is going to get real fuzzy, real quick, because I want no part of this, got me? I have a good job, a senior position at my company that I worked hard for, and I'm not going to let what happened back then mess things up."

"You've got to be kidding me. You were a cop," Sergio barked, but Mitch warned him off with a stern shake of the head. He tried to cool his growing anger. Mitch understood cops better than Sergio did and they needed information. He clamped his jaws together.

Mitch stared. "I know cops don't want to bad-mouth other cops, but there's a girl been dead for fifteen years who never got justice and we believe another woman was killed trying to uncover the truth. We'll keep you out of it as best we can, okay?"

"Not good enough. Like I said, I'll deny I ever said anything if you bring me into this again."

Mitch huffed out a breath. "Give us what you have, and you won't hear from us going forward."

Higgins pursed his lips. "All right. I don't have any hard evidence, but I'll share my impressions of what happened that night."

The mug of coffee shook slightly in Helen's hands. Sergio wanted to comfort her, but his own pulse was hammering through his system.

"The O'Brian investigation was botched from the get-go," Higgins said. "I was a new cop then, only a couple weeks out of the academy, but even I could see that. Farraday didn't secure the scene. He interviewed the teens in groups instead of individually. It was sloppy, unprofessional."

Sergio couldn't keep quiet any longer. "Why? What was his problem?"

Higgins toyed with his paper napkin. "Maybe he's just not a good cop."

"And maybe you aren't telling us the whole story," Sergio countered. "Why? Was he protecting one of the teens from blame?" He pictured the group, Justin, Gavin, Helen, Fiona and perhaps Allyson. The O'Brian family had money. Was it possible Farraday allowed Allyson to sneak away rather than take the blame for murdering her sister?

Higgins sucked in a breath. "He'd been drinking. I could smell it on his breath, over the mints he'd used to try to cover. I'd heard things before when he was assigned as my boss, rumors and such, that made me think he had a problem with alcohol. That night confirmed it."

Sergio wanted to reach across the table and shake the guy. "And you didn't say anything? Call in any other cops?"

"That's not how it works. Cops don't rat on cops, especially probationary guys who just sweated through twenty-six weeks of police academy training."

The blue code of silence. Sergio realized his hands were clenched into fists and he forced himself to take a breath. This was the only way they would get information and he couldn't blow it. "What did you think happened that night? What were your impressions?"

Higgins frowned. "The victim was hit on the back of the head with a blunt object, just like the coroner's report stated, but Farraday moved her body, and he didn't take photographs or wear gloves. There was water seeping in from somewhere, so by the time I arrived, there were about six inches of it pooling all around." He paused. "I read Farraday's report. He said he found her in the main tunnel and there were two others branching out east and west."

"Not factual?"

"Factual, but not complete. There was another opening, a hole, that you could access, that went down to a lower level. He didn't mention that in the report."

"You didn't offer a correction?" Mitch said.

"By the time we left the scene the tunnels were filling with water. I figured whatever evidence there might have been down there was flooded away anyway."

"All right," Mitch said. "Anything else? What about the kids' statements? Anything strike you as odd?"

"No, but like I said, he interviewed the boys together and the girls, which also violated protocols. They might have changed their stories." He shot a glance at Helen. "You were there, weren't you? Did we speak that night?"

She shook her head. "I only talked to Farraday. I might have seen you, but…it was all such a blur. I told Farraday that Fiona and I were in the western tunnel. We got lost for a long while, trying to find a way out—it was part of the game. We finally stumbled on an exit which let us out in the woods and we walked back."

"Did you see anybody on the way?" Sergio asked.

"No. By the time we got there, it was late, past midnight. Gavin and Justin were at Gavin's truck looking worried. They asked about Trish. I thought she was with them and they thought the same about us. She'd started out with the boys, but ducked out on them, trying to be funny, we guessed later. Justin and Gavin split up to search, but with no success. There was no answer when we called her, and we tried multiple times. We all went in together to look but the water was rising fast and we didn't see any sign of her so we finally called the police around 12:30 a.m. and Farraday came."

Sergio stared. "So none of you saw Trish's body?"

Helen shook her head. "Not until the fire department removed her on a stretcher just before we were all taken to the police station to make official statements."

"The water loosened a lot of debris which obscured her body, according to Farraday," Higgins said. "That's likely why the kids didn't see her when they looked in the chamber."

"After Farraday went in, it seemed like hours, but it was probably only forty-five minutes or so." Helen's voice was still flat, as if she was lost in the memories. "We were all expecting her to walk right out of those tunnels, laughing at how she'd tricked us. She loved a good prank." Helen sucked in a breath. "Instead, Farraday came out and told us she was dead. I thought it must be some sort of bad dream. I just could not believe what he was saying."

Higgins nodded. "I arrived about that time, a few minutes behind the volunteer fire department."

Dread tingled through Sergio. "Farraday was intoxicated when he went into the tunnels. Is it possible that Trish was alive at that point?"

"Alive?" Helen said. "What are you saying?"

He considered how much of his thoughts to reveal. "Maybe something went wrong. She fell, hurt herself, and he tried to save her but couldn't," Sergio said, slowly. "Or they got into some sort of argument and things got out of control."

Helen clutched her arms around herself. He tried to soften his dark musings. "Could be she realized he was drunk, pointed it out, said she would make a fuss, and he took offense, something like that."

"Far-fetched," Mitch said.

"I've heard stranger things," Uncle Gus put in.

Higgins ruminated. "Or, like I said, it could be just sloppy police work that he doesn't want held up for the world to see. He's trying to get a chief's job in another town, you know. A thing like botching a case due to a drinking problem would mean no department would touch him."

"Do you have any reason to suspect there was another person in the tunnels that night?" Uncle Gus said.

"Like Allyson O'Brian?" Higgins took in the surprised reactions. "I heard Fiona say she called Allyson's number when they were trying to locate her but there was no answer. I remember Gavin adding something to the effect that he was surprised she didn't follow Trish into the tunnels since she was furious at being excluded and lied to. The comment made an impression on me, but Farraday wrote in his report that when he contacted the O'Brians after Trish's body was transported, they mentioned having to call someone to stay with Allyson while they went to the hospital."

"So she was back by the time he made that call anyway. She could have been in the tunnels and home by then." Sergio bit back his irritation. More what-ifs without any proof.

Higgins pushed his coffee mug away. "So that's pretty much all I know."

"Pretty much?" Chad said.

"That means there's something more." Uncle Gus's tone was light, but he was not smiling. "Care to share anything else? Your silence might have prevented Trish

O'Brian's family from getting any justice fifteen years ago. If you can add anything else that might help now, I'd think you'd want to go ahead and do that, to settle your soul."

Sergio could see why Uncle Gus and Aunt Ginny had Helen's complete loyalty. They were good people, like his own parents, honest, God-fearing, salt-of-the-earth types as wide-open as their ranchland.

Higgins hesitated. "There is one more thing I can give you."

Sergio hoped it wasn't more vague suspicions. They already had plenty of those.

Higgins pulled a thumb drive from his pocket. "Like I said, Farraday didn't take many pictures of the crime scene." He smacked the device on the table. "But I did."

Sergio almost bolted from his chair. "Photos?"

"My personal photos. I didn't share them since that would make Farraday look bad, but I always hung on to them, waiting, I suppose, for this moment when somebody would ask questions. I didn't take many pictures of Trish's body, since they were loading her up as I arrived. These are shots of the area where she was found and the west and east tunnels and some of the adjoining passageway through the hole, whatever I could get before the water level rose too high."

He got up. "Now you've got the photos and I've done what I can. Don't contact me again. I hope you find your killer."

As he watched Higgins go, Sergio experienced a rising hope that maybe they'd finally gotten the break they needed to do just that.

THIRTEEN

Helen stared at the thumb drivc. Could it actually hold the identity of Trish's killer? She knew in her bones that the answer to that mystery would also lead them right to Fiona's murderer.

Mitch slid his laptop onto the table and inserted the thumb drive. It took a few moments for the pictures to load. Chad and Mitch sat elbow to elbow, while Helen, Sergio, Aunt Ginny and Gus stood behind. After an interminable wait, thumbnails of the photos began to pop up, one by one. Mitch sat patiently until the upload was complete before he clicked on the first one.

The photo was dim, a small chamber with shadowed exits on both sides. Helen's stomach balled up. There was a tarp-covered bundle lying on the floor. Trish. Her throat clogged, and she felt as though she was right back at that horrible night, the scent of the damp tunnels strong in her memory. Sergio's arm went around her shoulder, holding her steady.

"I'm sorry," he said, lips brushing her cheek. "I know this is hard."

She clamped her lips together and blinked furiously. *Do it for Trish and Fiona.* She allowed her gaze to wander across the screen. "You can see the archway there, which is the one Fiona and I decided on. And there's the one leading east."

"How did you get in?" Mitch asked.

"Gavin cut the lock with bolt cutters. It was trespassing, of course, but that didn't stop us." How she wished it had. Sergio's grip tightened.

"You were kids. Kids do dumb things," he said. "I sure did my share."

She cleared her throat. "The challenge was whichever team could find a way out of the tunnels without doubling back through the front entrance would be the winner. We were supposed to rendezvous at Gavin's car by midnight." How childish it sounded now, like a dream from the past. *A deadly dream.*

They scrolled through several more photos and it was clear that the water level was rising in each one. It was the next series of pictures that snapped Helen to attention.

"That must be the hole Higgins was talking about." The gap was nothing more than a jagged circle of broken cement. The following picture showed a damp tunnel sloping downward. Higgins must have climbed through the hole and taken a few steps before he snapped the picture. She could see his shadow reflected off the water in the photo.

"Can you zoom in?" Sergio said.

Mitch did so. They stared at the screen. "So if Allyson, or someone else crept in and killed her, this is likely how they got out without being seen by the others."

Sergio grunted. "And Farraday never even investigated it."

Helen peered closer. "What's that?"

Sergio followed her pointed finger, squinting. "I see it. Something glinting there, something metallic."

Mitch zoomed the image as much as he could before the screen became grainy. "It looks like a section of pipe, resting high up on that stone ledge."

Helen felt sick. "Like the blunt object the coroner said was used to kill Trish?"

Mitch stared at the screen. "Should have been taken by the police, tested for prints, blood, etc. if Farraday had handled things properly. At least the tunnels were locked up again so hopefully it's still there."

Sergio straightened. "I can check it out."

"We'll go too. If you do find it, we'll leave it and call in the cops," Mitch warned.

"Not Farraday," Sergio said.

"No. I'll call a cop I trust from Sand Dune. We'll keep it on the downlow, but I will inform Danny Patron before we attempt this. Since it's public land, we'll need him to help arrange with the parks department to give us access. They won't be keen on the idea since the tunnels are likely flooded at this time of year. I'll get working on that right now and let you know when we have a green light."

"Fair enough," Sergio said.

"I need to go check on things at the lodge, but I can get free any time after that," Helen said.

"No need for you to come..." Mitch started, but Helen was already reaching for her jacket, Jingles at her heels, striding to the door after a word for Aunt Ginny.

He huffed out a breath that made Sergio want to laugh. "I don't think any of us are going to talk her out of joining in."

"Can't say as I blame her," Chad said. "Those tunnels changed her life, all their lives."

"And a killer went free," Sergio mused. "Wouldn't it be incredible if it turned out to be Trish's sister?"

"We don't know that." Chad's eyes sparked. "How about we don't throw around any more accusations until we have proof?" He stalked away in search of Helen.

Sergio raised an eyebrow to Mitch. "Did I hit a nerve?"

"Chad's father was accused of negligence," he said, closing his laptop.

"I heard that. Drinking while captaining a vessel."

Mitch gave him a sharp glance. "Chad believes his dad was framed."

Sergio arched a brow. "Blood alcohol levels were wrong?"

His expression darkened, and Sergio imagined it was the look he'd given to plenty of criminals in his tenure as a US marshal. "Haven't you seen from this case that things aren't always what they appear to be?"

Sergio nodded in concession. "Yeah. Does Chad think there was a dirty cop involved in his situation too?"

"Let's just say it ruined Chad's family. He has a right to be sensitive." Sergio got the message. *You're not family. Butt out.* He understood. Until a few days ago he hadn't wanted to be involved with Helen or any of her family either.

Chad's cold-shoulder attitude became suddenly more understandable. Sergio resolved to be more sensitive about his remarks. Sensitive? Him? This weird little town really was messing with his mind.

Mitch headed into the kitchen, leaving Sergio alone with Uncle Gus and Aunt Ginny who walked him to the door.

Ginny offered a smile, Gus's arm resting on her waist.

"We all have different kinds of hurts," she said. "Chad just hasn't come to terms with his yet."

Something about their genuine warmth inspired him to confide. "I'm not sure I've come to terms with mine either."

Ginny clucked. "We get it."

Gus nodded thoughtfully. "Hope you'll find some peace for yourself and your girls here in Driftwood."

"I will when I catch Fiona's murderer."

Ginny cocked her head. "And if you don't?"

"I will, and the killer will pay."

"We hope so," Ginny said, "but, honey, if you don't get the vengeance you're looking for, what will you do then?"

The thought startled him. Go on living with the angry hole burning away in his gut?

Ginny settled against her husband's side. "I've never had any children of my own, but I've been around plenty of them, and one thing I've noticed is that kids learn what is and isn't important from the people closest to them, no matter how much the grown-ups try to hide it."

The statement hit him like a backhanded slap. What was he modeling? Would the girls learn to seek vengeance for the wrongs in their lives above all other things? Had he shown them that justice was more important than love? The Lord? Surely he'd kept the simmering rage from them. Hadn't he?

...no matter how much the grown-ups try to hide it...

"Be careful, Sergio," Aunt Ginny said. He wondered if she was talking about the tunnel excursion or about how he was handling his life. Both, he decided. But they didn't understand how it felt to lose a sister, to know that her killer could very well be walking around Driftwood enjoying all the happiness that rightfully belonged to her. Plenty of people wanted him to quit.

Gavin's wife, who warned them off the investigation.

Justin and Gavin, so close to all the danger that had occurred at the lodge.

Allyson and her simmering hatred of her sister.

The police chief who'd supposedly discovered Trish's body.

Everyone had their secrets in Driftwood, he thought.

But there was only one he cared about. He would catch the killer, and the girls would always know their mother had gotten the justice she deserved.

I won't stop, Fiona, not until your killer pays.

Mind settled, he strode outside.

Helen's phone rang just after the dinner service, but it was not the number she expected. After a calming breath, she stepped out onto the front porch of the lodge and answered. "Hi, Liam."

The connection was crackly, but she heard her brother's every word, his Southern drawl pronounced, the drawl she'd worked so hard to tame in herself. "What is going on and please tell me you're staying out of it?"

"How are you? Is Maggie feeling better?"

"Speak up, okay? I can't hear you."

It was not the connection, most likely, but the otosclerosis that was gradually rendering him deaf. She spoke louder. "I hope you two had a good time."

"Phenomenal, and so far she hasn't decided she made a mistake marrying me."

"Glad to hear that."

"We're trying to get a flight home, but everything's grounded due to storms. And don't try to distract me with small talk. What is going on? Mitch and Chad haven't explained everything to my satisfaction."

She told him the abbreviated version. He cut her off toward the end.

"Go stay with Aunt Ginny and Uncle Gus."

"You should add *please* to the end of an order, but I'm fine here. I've got cameras and brothers and Sergio and Jingles."

He snorted. "I don't know this Sergio guy, but Jingles couldn't scare away a blindfolded, three-legged butterfly."

She laughed. "I'm perfectly safe and I won't do anything dangerous, I promise."

"That's not good enough. I'm coming home as soon as I can, but in the meantime..."

She sighed. It would do no good to talk him out of it, but she tried anyway. "It's your honeymoon, Liam. What about Maggie?"

"Maggie is itching to get back to the lodge. She's got all kinds of ideas for the menu."

"Tell her I can't wait to hear about them. I started a new spreadsheet for the fall season."

"I'm sure you did, and flowcharts and line plots all properly footnoted in three different colors." He was quiet a moment. "Seriously, Helen. Don't let that guilt you're hanging on to put you at risk. You were not to blame for Fiona. If Sergio's making you feel like..."

"He's not, Liam. Truly." She saw Mitch and Sergio walking up the porch steps. "I have to go now, okay?"

"But you haven't told me..."

"Goodbye, Liam. I'll see you soon. Give my love to Maggie." She clicked off.

Mitch grinned as he approached. "Liam?"

She closed her eyes for a moment. "He hasn't commandeered a plane or anything so far, so that's a win."

Chad joined them next, a rope tossed over his shoulder. "Brushed down your horses," he told Helen. "Took me twice as long since Liam called me every five minutes."

"Called me also when I was moving the herd," Mitch said. "I finally told him I was gonna block his number if he didn't stop pestering."

"That's right about when he started in on me," Chad said. "He's probably on the line with Aunt Ginny right now."

"She can handle him," Mitch said. "I got permission, thanks to Danny, and a key from the parks department to explore the tunnels, but the clerk nicely told me if anything happens to us, it's not their fault. He said there's a reason the area is off-limits."

"Understood," Sergio said. "I've got flashlights and hard hats in my SUV."

"Where'd you come up with those?" Helen asked.

He waved an airy hand. "I'm resourceful."

Mitch rolled his eyes. "All right, Mr. Resourceful, we're all set then, but it's gonna have to wait until first thing tomorrow."

"Why?" Helen and Sergio both blurted.

Chad laughed.

Mitch was unmoved by their outburst. "Because it's almost dark, and we're gonna use some common sense here for a change. Sunrise is at 7:25 a.m. tomorrow morning. We'll gather at 6:30 a.m., saddle up, Chad will ride an ATV over from the ranch. I'll be here at the lodge tonight on guard duty."

"But..." Helen started.

Mitch stretched his long frame until his back popped. "I hope you're going to bed early tonight, Helen. Save me the trouble of following you all over every corner of this lodge."

"I was thinking about searching the basement again for that memory book."

"Chad and I combed through it all again. Nothing there in the way of a memory book."

Helen groaned. "I can picture it in my mind's eye, pink cover with a heart on the front and Fiona's loopy cursive spelling out the captions for each photo. I never would have thrown it away, like Allyson did."

"Allegedly," Sergio added.

She pursed her lips. "So where is it? And what if it's the clue we need to solve the murders?"

"Tomorrow may yield some clues of its own," Sergio said. "To be cautious, let's not make it public knowledge what we're doing. Agreed?"

They did.

"All right. I'm off to help with the dessert service, and then I'm going straight to my room to work on some promotional materials," she announced.

"Good." Mitch opened the lodge door for her. "I'll be right there standing alongside the pies, sis."

"Peach cobbler," she corrected.

"Even better."

Jingles trotted through the open door before Helen had a chance to. She shot an anxious look over her shoulder. The shadows were growing as the day gave way to evening. A cold breeze swept past her, chilling her skin and getting inside her.

She wondered if Burnette was out there, waiting for

his chance to get inside the lodge again, to make his way up the stairs and…

Sergio touched her shoulder and she twitched.

"I'm watching from the cabin and I've got the camera outside your bedroom transmitting visuals to my phone as well as the front desk. No one will hurt you."

She tried for a cheeky grin, but the tremble of her lips probably negated her bravado. "Promise?"

He didn't smile, increasing the pressure on her shoulder slightly, allowing his fingers to brush her neck which added to the goose bumps.

"I promise," he said just before she stepped through the door.

FOURTEEN

It was dark at six thirty in the morning when Sergio chugged some coffee and hauled on his jacket. The caffeine provided a welcome jolt, since he'd done regular checks of the grounds and the camera feed all night. In between checks, he'd gone over the cold case file which Danny Patron had provided Mitch and agreed to allow Sergio to see, as well. Sergio imagined Farraday was probably furious about the disclosure, but there was nothing much he could do about it. That notion put a smile on his face.

Another half cup of coffee did not rouse him completely. As a younger man he'd been a rock-solid sleeper, which proved a problem since he'd discovered that tiny children tended to have problematic situations in the dead of night. When they'd gotten old enough, he'd fastened a whistle next to their beds for them to blow on if they needed him. His pride over his ingenious parenting hack vanished when the first midnight blast nearly gave him a heart attack. He realized he'd forgotten to pack the whistles when they'd come to Driftwood. Another oversight due to his hyperfocus on solving the case. A noise made him jump and he whirled to see Lucy standing barefoot in the kitchen, sucking on her three middle fingers and twisting the sleeve of her pink nightie.

He dropped to a knee. "What are you doing out of bed, buttercup?"

She didn't answer. He settled to the floor and took her up onto his lap. "Your feet are cold," he said, rubbing the soles. She slid her skinny arms inside his jacket sleeves, making him gasp. "Hands are cold too."

He held her and rocked her from side to side until she pointed to her bunny, lying forgotten in the corner of the kitchen.

"Oh, is that what you were missing?"

She nodded as he scooped her and the bunny up and bundled her back to bed next to her snoozing sister who clutched her matching bunny. He kept meaning to find replicas of those toys in case the unthinkable happened and they somehow lost one. That notion made his blood run cold. He remembered driving three hours to double back to the pizza joint where Lucy had dropped her toy one time. He'd had to resist the urge to hug the brusque owner who'd rescued Bunny from the floor.

"Go to sleep now, Lucy. I'll be back soon." She clung to him for just a moment before she sank into the bed and he covered her up to the chin. As he tiptoed out, he thought about what Aunt Ginny had said.

Children learned what was important from the people around them. It was his number-one mission to catch Fiona's killer and he'd never allowed himself to consider any other outcomes. What would happen if he failed? Could he leave Driftwood and his vengeance behind forever? Could he actually give up his relentless search? Would Fiona want him to? Would God? The questions bunched up together until he felt paralyzed by them.

He sank onto his knees outside their bedroom door and pressed his forehead to the painted wood. "Lord…" he started, but the words stuck in his throat. He tried again. "Lord, help me to love them the right way. If it means giving up, You're going to have to help me with that too." It hurt to say it; it hurt to think it.

He stayed there a moment more until the pain passed, gradually soaking in the quiet of the house, the knowledge that Lucy and Laurel were safe and warm and content for the time being. Feeling lighter inside, he let himself out of the cabin and met Helen and Mitch at the corral. The horses were saddled and ready. The windows of the lodge were dark, except for landscape lighting and the glow of the lobby.

As he got onto his horse, he thought he saw the flicker of a flashlight beam coming from the trees behind. He whirled the gelding and trotted over. Helen and Mitch joined him.

"What?" Helen's face was barely visible.

He related what he'd thought he'd seen. "Maybe I was wrong."

Mitch eyed the sky. "Let's get going. The sooner we're out of sight of the lodge the better. Chad's already there on the ATV. All quiet."

Helen appeared composed, but he let Mitch lead the way and eased his horse next to hers. The trail was thickly wooded, the trees weeping moisture down on them. The smell of eucalyptus and wet earth hung heavy in his nostrils. "Get any sleep?"

"Not much. Jingles slept fine, though. He snores like a freight train."

"Where is he?"

"I left him with Evonne."

Sergio turned at a sound behind them and smiled. "I guess he didn't get that memo."

Jingles scurried along the path and fell into step next to them with a friendly tail wag and a yip for Helen.

"How does he do that?" she mused.

"Maybe Liam put him up to it. Did they talk on the phone any of the last twelve times he called you?"

She giggled, and he was glad he'd cheered her, though her smile slipped away a moment later as the trail pinched tighter, squeezed by piles of granite.

"It's…strange thinking about going back down there."

"You don't have to."

"Yes, I do," she said. "This is not going to be over until we know for sure if there's any evidence. I'm a witness from that night."

The most reliable witness… Fiona and Trish dead. Justin and Gavin steeped in their busy lives. And Allyson…? Had she been there that night?

"I wish I could think where the memory book might be."

If it hadn't been destroyed or lost. More questions than answers. He considered the what-ifs Aunt Ginny proposed. He cleared his throat. "A lot could have happened to the crime scene. It's been years. It's possible, as much as I don't like to admit it, that we aren't going to find anything. I'm trying to decide how to handle that."

She looked startled. "Will you be able to?"

The answer came from someplace deep, a spot he'd not plumbed before until just that moment. "I never thought so, but I've been reminded lately I've got two girls who are looking to me to show them how to live in this world even when there's disappointment and injustice. I've got to try to show them that, though I'm not sure exactly how."

He looked at her as the sun began to peek through the canopy of trees, gilding her hair, awakening the green of her eyes and highlighting the gentle sincerity in her smile. "Even if I can't give up on getting their mama justice, I can show them there are people here who are pretty amazing at helping us with life's rough patches."

People like you.

The thought startled him.

She smiled again and turned away. Why did his feelings become softer, gentler when he was with her? Why did he long to be a better man, a better father, because he knew she would be proud of those things? When they were together he felt free, like he was swimming in warm ocean waters.

Would you knock it off, Sergio? All this drama and danger were messing with his emotions. Friendship with Helen was something he hadn't bargained for and anything more than that... He cut the thoughts off as the horses crested the rocky slope and the entrance to the tunnels became visible. They tied the horses near the ATV.

Chad handed them each a hard hat with a headlamp and a flashlight.

Mitch unfastened the heavy padlock which opened with a bone-chilling squeak. They were assaulted by a waft of dank, cold air, heavy with the scent of mildew.

Helen shivered, though she was wearing a nylon jacket.

He flicked on his own flashlight. "Are you sure you're ready for this?"

"Not sure, but I'm doing it anyway."

They pressed, single file, into the darkness, Chad in

front with Mitch, then Sergio and Helen bringing up the rear. The heavy overhead beams were slick with moisture. One freezing drop hit his neck and rolled down under his shirt collar. The place was silent as a tomb except for the incessant dripping. Inside the entrance they aimed the lights around to acclimate themselves.

"Western tunnel," Mitch said, using his beam of light to mark the entrance. "The one the girls took. And the eastern tunnel, there."

Sergio noted the damp under his boots. "Groundwater seepage," he said. "But at least it's not flooded here." He walked to the far wall, careful not to bang his forehead on a low-hanging rock. He played his flashlight through the darkness, searching for the hole they'd seen in the photos Frank Higgins had taken. It took him a moment to find it, his light catching the gap broken through the stone, no more than two feet across and eighteen inches from the ground.

"That's where I'm headed," he said. If the pipe was still there, and it was the murder weapon, there would be DNA. At last, a solid lead amidst the sea of dead ends. Picking his way around some rock, he knelt and peered into the maw. Instantly he knew the situation had changed. With a groan he extricated himself to find the others staring at him.

"Status?" Mitch said.

"Flooded," Sergio informed them. "There's probably ten feet of water there now, much deeper than when Higgins photographed. Not surprising, I guess, since it's pitched downward and it's been a wet winter."

Chad thumbed back his hard hat. "So what's the problem? You're a diver, right?"

Sergio grinned. "At last, some respect for my ferocious skills."

Jingles turned suddenly, raced out the entrance, barking madly.

"Jingles," Helen called, but the dog beelined out into the rising sun. Was he after a squirrel? Or a human? Sergio thought of the flick of light he'd seen in the woods behind the lodge. What if they'd been tracked? Or worse, if someone had gotten here ahead of them?

At the same moment, Sergio noticed the coil of wires protruding from a little black box jammed into a crevice in the ceiling. His brain screamed a warning before his mouth caught up.

"Explosive," he yelled, shoving Helen toward the tunnel entrance.

She stumbled but kept her footing. They all lunged in the same direction a moment too late.

The bomb detonated with an earsplitting boom.

Helen fell forward, tumbling to the rocky ground as a plume of dust billowed from the tunnel behind her. Her hard hat went flying. The ground under her palms vibrated from the released energy. Mitch grabbed her hand and hauled her to her feet, propelling her away from the tumult.

"Stay here," he barked.

She bent over, sucking in a breath. Jingles was suddenly with her, licking her face, his paws scrabbling against her thighs. "All right—I'm okay," she said, relieved that the dog had not been there when the explosion occurred.

She turned around to see Chad following Mitch back into the mine, but she did not see Sergio. Her breath caught. Where had he been during the moment of the blast? Behind her, and near the hole. Panic nearly paralyzed her, but she forced herself to approach the opening, one shaky step at a time. Dust stung her eyes but gradually it began to settle.

What if Sergio hadn't gotten clear? Her thoughts raced in crazed circles. How would it feel to know he was gone? How would she ever tell his little girls? Now her breath completely froze in her lungs as the dust swirled and coalesced, concealing the opening. Two steps farther and she heard movement.

Mitch and Chad appeared through the entrance supporting Sergio between them. She almost whooped aloud, dogging their steps as they sat him on a rock.

"I think he's okay," Mitch said.

Sergio nodded. "Just dandy."

Mitch clapped him on the back, releasing a puff of dust from his shirt. "Chad, bring your light and let's see if we can assess the tunnel damage." They returned to the entrance.

Sergio shook himself like a great bear, loosening more of the dirt which covered him in a coat of gray. Helen did not trust herself to speak over the keen sense of relief, so thick it nearly choked her.

"Man, my ears are ringing something fierce," he said.

She threw her arms around him, tears flowing hot and mingling with the grit on his cheeks. His arms encircled her waist.

"I'm all right," he said into her neck.

She pulled away so she could look at him. "Are you sure? Really sure? Something might be cracked or lacerated or…squashed."

He gave her a bemused chuckle, pulled her close and kissed her on the mouth. The connection sparked warm spirals that floated through her body, pushing away the terror, eclipsing everything but the comfort she felt in that kiss. She twined her arms around him and held him close, wondering why she had never felt this way before with any other man. How right it felt to be close to him, to share with him, but how could that be? *You're kissing Fiona's brother*, her brain blared.

She pulled back suddenly, breathless, seeing her own startled expression mirrored in his eyes. Mechanically she brushed off the grit from his shoulders and flicked away the dust from his hair until he grabbed her hand.

"I upset you. I'm sorry," he said. "Couldn't help myself."

"Oh, no problem," she babbled. "It was a reaction, is all. You know, to the explosion. It was an explosion, right?" she chattered, still feeling the cascade of sparks trickling through her nerves. "Not an earthquake?"

"Affirmative on the explosion," Mitch said, as he and Chad rejoined them. "Remote triggered, by a cell phone probably, so someone was in range and watching. Must have gotten in another way since the lock was intact when we got here. I think Jingles heard whoever it was which is why he took off."

Helen bent to give him a good ear rub. "If he hadn't, we might have all been stuck in there."

"Or squashed," Sergio said, smiling.

She ignored him, trying to forget the butterflies in her stomach from their kiss. "Extra dog cookies for you tonight, Jingles."

Jingles snaked a wet tongue along her cheek.

"Farraday's on his way," Mitch said. "You can imagine how thrilled he is, considering he didn't know we were having this little adventure."

Sergio groaned. "We knew he'd find out eventually,

but I was hoping we'd have some evidence to show before he got wind of it."

"Looks like that's going to be a trick and a half to pull off," Chad said.

Helen jerked a look at him as he explained. "Entrance beam collapsed. Look."

She stood, stomach sinking in dismay. The thick beam was lying fractured on the ground, underneath a pile of rock which had broken away in the explosion.

Jingles barked, and all of them tensed at the sound of someone approaching.

"Too soon for Farraday," Mitch said.

Sergio got to his feet and stepped next to Mitch, edging in front of Helen.

Helen swallowed. Had the person who planted the explosive intended to scare them…or kill them? And was he coming back to finish the job?

FIFTEEN

Sergio's temples throbbed as he watched the gap in the trees. His ears rang, a leftover of the explosion. Allyson O'Brian came into view, astride a sleek dark horse with a white patch on his muzzle. Her fiery red hair was covered by a dark knit cap that matched her black jacket. She certainly wasn't dressed to be visible. He thought she tensed a bit at the sight of them before she led the horse closer.

"What happened?" she demanded. "I heard a boom."

"There was an explosion," he said, watching her face carefully. Her frown didn't give away any deeper emotion, like disappointment that they were still alive, just wariness and something else he couldn't identify. "What are you doing here?"

"Tom at the convention brought Fairytale here for me to ride. I'm thinking about buying her. What exploded?" Her eyes narrowed, sweeping the scene. "The tunnel entrance?"

"Yes. Did you see anyone on your way up here?" Mitch asked.

"A guy, short, with curly hair was walking back down the trail after I heard the noise. I asked him if he knew what happened. He laughed and said he didn't hear a thing and kept on going."

"I'll update Farraday." Mitch walked quickly to the high point where he could get a signal and made the call.

Allyson looked behind them at the ruined entrance. "Why are you here? I mean, why do you want to go back into those tunnels?" She gripped the reins tightly.

"Following up on a lead," Sergio said. "Does that bother you?"

She shook her head, but her expression was hard. "I don't care what you do, but I just don't see why you'd want to go back inside. The police already investigated."

"They might have missed some things," Sergio said. "We've gotten some more information that could help us find out what really happened to your sister."

Her mouth tightened. "She's dead, that's what happened. Nothing can change that."

Sergio heard the barest flicker of dismay which she concealed quickly. He saw the flash of pain on Helen's face as Mitch rejoined them.

"Don't look so shocked," she said to Helen. "It's not like we were close. She wanted to spend time with you and her other friends more than me."

Helen flinched. "I'm sorry, Allyson. I know you felt excluded. I didn't mean to get between you and your sister."

Allyson shrugged. "You didn't. She was too busy running the other way to care about who she left behind. I'm taking Fairytale back now. He needs to be brushed down."

Chad nodded. "Nice animal. Gonna buy him?"

Her manner thawed a bit. "Maybe. He's sensitive."

"Typical for a thoroughbred," Chad said. "Likes a

light hand and seat. Tom Rourke's a family friend. He wouldn't steer you wrong."

"Yeah," she allowed a small smile which made her look altogether younger. "Fairytale wouldn't work for a beginner, but we might make a good pair." As she turned the horse around, she stopped for a moment, looking back at the settling cloud of dust. The silence was peppered with the sound of rocks continuing to fall from what had been the tunnel entrance, adding to the detritus.

"The curly-haired guy," Allyson said abruptly. "I've seen him before, with Fiona."

Sergio's mouth fell open. "What? Where?"

"That same day she came to see me about three years back. I was in town that morning, picking up some horse vitamins from the vet and I saw her. She saw me too, crossed the street to talk to me. That's when she arranged to come see me at my house."

"Where was she when she spotted you? What store was she visiting?" He could almost not get the words out fast enough.

"A dive shop. She was talking with the owner while he swept his front stoop."

Why would Fiona have been visiting a dive shop? They'd done some diving together, but why would she be interested at that time, during her brief visit to Driftwood? Allyson looked like she wanted to say more.

"The guy," she said slowly, "the one I passed today on my way up here, he was there at the shop too."

Sergio felt the revelation ripple through him like the blast that had obliterated the tunnel entrance. "Did he speak to my sister?"

"I don't know. Not when I was looking. Anyway, that's all I have to tell you."

"Thank you for your help," he said.

She shook her head. "Don't thank me. I'm not interested in helping anyone dig up what happened that night. Like I said, dead is dead." She led the horse away.

Sergio stared after her, nerves buzzing. "As soon as Farraday's done with us, I'm going to talk to the dive-shop owner."

"Do you trust the information?" Mitch flicked a look in the direction Allyson had taken.

"You think she's lying?" Helen said.

"I'm not saying that, but she was in the right place to set off the explosion herself. You can get a signal just down the path where she came from. Her cell phone was in her back pocket."

Helen blew out a breath. "I can't believe she'd do that."

Sergio considered. "Why would she give us the dive-shop guy then? If she'd just tried to blow us up?"

"Diversion," Mitch said. "She had an opportunity to tell you before when you met with her, but somehow she didn't happen to recall the detail at that time."

"It's a memory from three years ago," Helen said. "I can see why her recollections would be sketchy. Mine are too."

Sergio was silent a moment. "Mitch is right to be cautious. The last time we had an encounter with Allyson, we almost died on a mountain road."

"And this time..." Helen looked back to the pile of rubble. She didn't have to finish the sentence. He allowed himself a moment to think about the kiss. Helen was drawing closer to him than he'd ever allowed a woman before. Part of him longed for another kiss, but he couldn't indulge that incomprehensible thought. It was too dangerous to let her continue in the investigation and way too disturbing to have her close.

Was it her physical safety he was worried about?

Or the unsettling notion that the more time he spent with Helen, the more he craved her presence. It was a bigger dose of confusion than he could deal with on top of trying to raise two very befuddling daughters.

Solve the case. Keep Helen safe. Give your daughters a good life. Those had to be his priorities. There was no room for any kind of a permanent relationship with a woman, especially a woman who'd been his sister's best friend.

Think like an investigator, he told himself, as Faraday came huffing up the hill along with another cop. As soon as he could, he would head to the dive shop and get some answers. A secondary avenue suddenly dawned on him, a plan he would not divulge to any of them. It would take finesse, since he'd have to get some information from Helen while keeping her in the dark.

He recalled the concern in those vivid green eyes, the softness of her arms around his neck, as if they were perfectly fitted for each other. As he watched her stroking Jingles behind the ears, worry and strength visible in the graceful lines of her posture, he knew that was going to be the most difficult challenge of all.

Helen, Sergio and Chad returned their horses to the corral, while Mitch stayed behind ostensibly to provide more information, but Helen suspected he was intending to supervise the investigation into the explosion. The tunnels were now impassable, at least for the moment. Another dead end? The expression might have taken on a different meaning altogether if Sergio hadn't gotten out in time. She shivered.

Chad took the reins from Helen and Sergio. Jingles assumed his position at Helen's side.

"I can brush down the horse," Sergio said with a touch of pique.

Chad stroked the gelding's mane. "No offense, but I can do it better."

Sergio gave him a look, then broke into a wry smile. "I'm thinking that's probably truth telling rather than boasting."

Helen laughed. "Yes, it is. Nobody understands horses better than Chad. He wants to start a nonprofit to connect struggling veterans with rescued horses as a way of helping them both."

"I've got all kinds of respect for that," Sergio said.

Chad gave him a nod of acknowledgment. "There's a need. My dad is a veteran." Chad led the horses away before Sergio could ask any questions. "Don't go anywhere alone," he said over his shoulder.

"I won't," Helen said.

"He doesn't talk much," Sergio observed as Chad moved off.

She was going to defend her brother, offer an explanation, but Sergio waved her off. "Nothing wrong with that," he said. "He shows what kind of man he is by his actions. That's good enough for me."

For whatever reason, it pleased her that Sergio seemed to have a level of admiration for Chad. "Liam is fond of saying Chad makes less noise than a fly landing on a feather duster."

Sergio chuckled. "That works too." They walked away from the corral, disturbing tiny ice crystals that had formed overnight on the fallen leaves and had yet to melt in the late morning sun. "I've got to get a shower and then I am going to the dive shop. You should stay..."

"Here and tend to my lodge duties. Nice try. I'll go check in and be at your cabin in twenty minutes. If you leave without me, I'll drive myself."

"Wait," he said, catching her wrist and turning her around to face him. "This is getting serious."

Suddenly her senses tingled, and the words took on a different meaning as she felt afresh the explosion, the rising cloud of debris that had obscured him from sight, the wild firing of her emotions when he'd kissed her. *Getting serious.*

She flashed a cheerful smile. "You're the one who almost got caught in the explosion. Maybe you should stay here and tend to the lodge."

He didn't smile back, his thumbs brushing the tender place where her pulse pounded. Could he feel it?

"Helen," he said, low and deep. Her gaze dropped to his mouth and for a moment she half feared and half wished he would pull her close for another kiss. Instead he cleared his throat and released his grip. "If it was Burnette, he has a really good reason to keep us out of the tunnels, or he's been paid by someone with a really good reason. It's bold, planting an explosive. Desperate. I don't want you hurt."

"Why do you care so much?" The words came out before she could think better of it. She felt like kicking herself for putting him on the spot in such a way. What was she, a high schooler?

He didn't seem surprised, or flustered, just thoughtful. "You were my sister's best friend," he said simply.

Her stomach twisted and the tension she'd felt a moment before leaked out of her, leaving behind exhaustion that turned her limbs to lead. What had she expected him to say? What had she wanted him to say? For the very first time she wondered what Fiona would think about the maelstrom of feelings she experienced being so near her brother. Before, she'd thought Fiona would be sad that Sergio kept her out of his life, the girls' lives. Now what would she make of the fact that they'd kissed? The air seemed chillier than it had before, carrying the faintest scent of bacon from the brunch being served in the cozy dining hall.

My sister's best friend.

Whatever their relationship was now or in the future, she would always and forever be Fiona's best friend. Ironic that the fact that brought them together would always keep them the perfect distance apart. She could not summon a smile this time. "I'll see you in a few minutes, okay?" Not waiting for his reply, she called to Jingles, and hurried back toward work and the safety of tasks to be completed, the comfort of a checklist.

SIXTEEN

Sergio finally got the last of the grit washed away and played jump rope with the girls for a while, keeping an eye on the lodge entrance, waiting for Helen to emerge. When they tired of the game, he brought them inside.

"Are you off on another mission?" Betty said, looking over from the counter where she was spreading peanut butter and jelly on slices of bread.

"Just tracking down some leads."

"With Helen?"

"Yes," he said, hoping his tone would discourage what he suspected was coming next.

"I like Helen."

"I like her too."

"And the girls like her."

He held up a finger. "Betty, I know where you're going with this, and it's not going to happen."

"Why not?"

"I can think of a whole lot of reasons."

"Name two."

He gaped, heat rising to his face. "First, she was Fiona's best friend."

"Which proves you both have the good sense to value Helen's excellent qualities."

He plowed onward. "And second… I've got two girls to raise and that's a big enough job."

"All the more reason to find a partner who can love these girls as much as you do."

He stood there, the jump rope in his hand and a girl clamped to each of his legs. "I appreciate your help, but it's not going to happen. There's just too much…baggage."

Betty added sliced apples to each plate and carried them to the table. "Sergio, everyone's got baggage. If God gives you someone to help share the load, you'd be a fool to turn them away. End of sermon."

And then she herded the girls to the bathroom for the premeal handwashing, leaving him standing there, mouth open to reply.

Betty had a way of tying things up into neat bundles, probably a result of her days as an accountant. But this was a messy matter with old hurts and tangled loyalties that couldn't be sorted out quite so neatly.

The case. That was what he needed to focus on. Putting Betty's well-meaning interference out of his mind, he got the keys to the loaner truck and waited for Helen.

"Jingles went with Chad back to the ranch for the afternoon chores," she said when she joined him. Something about her tone was overly brusque and he wondered if he'd hurt her feelings earlier. But he'd been right to try to get her to stay behind, hadn't he? Liam the Green Beret would certainly have said so and he knew Chad and Mitch would be happy if she didn't set foot outside the lodge without an armed platoon.

As they drove to the downtown area, he tried to nudge from her the information he needed.

"Back in high school, you went into the tunnels together, you, Justin, Gavin, Trish and Fiona. Then you split up, right?"

"Yes." She still did not quite meet his eye. "That was the game. Find a different way out."

He spooled the question out slowly, casually. "You said you and Fiona emerged in the woods and hiked back to where the car was parked."

She nodded absently. "We were thinking of ways to tease the boys. Gavin was easy—he was the quarterback on our high school football team and they were dead last in the league. It was mean, to tease him about that, since he tried so hard." She bit her lip. "We intended to razz Justin about his flashy ring, which we said made him look like a gangster. That was probably not very nice either, since it was a family ring." She sighed. "I wish we could go back and change some things, be kinder, notice people like Allyson."

He was momentarily derailed from his question at the regret in her voice. "We all wish that. I was pretty nasty to a guy who stole a girl from me, or at least that's what I told myself he did. In reality, she liked him better—he was smart, had good manners and wanted to talk about things other than boats and diving so she probably made the right choice. I didn't forgive him though, talked smack to the guys about him. It was petty and juvenile."

Her expression softened into a smile. "You mean you weren't always a responsible-adult type?"

"I don't think I really grew up completely until I became a father all of a sudden." He sighed. "Probably still have some growing up to do." He guided the truck along a quiet street, lined with old shingle-roofed homes, then turned down a side road that would lead to the main drag.

"So you found a way out into the woods. In which direction did you hike back to meet the boys? Do you recall?"

He should have known she would see through his smokescreen. She rounded on him. "You want to find another way in."

He tried to look innocent. "Just making conversation."

"No, you're not. You're looking for the second access into the tunnels. But they might not be safe. They could collapse now that there's been an explosion, and besides, the whole place could be underwater."

"Underwater is not a problem for me."

Her lovely green eyes rounded. "Sergio, you're not going to go back in there."

"I will if I can."

Now it was her turn to feign innocence. "And what if I can't remember the location of the place we came out?"

"Then I'll be forced to hike all over hither and yon." He winked at her. "I'm fine with hither, but I think yon might be tricky to find."

She groaned. "You are a problem."

"I will not deny it."

They pulled up at the curb of the Wave Life Fishing and Dive shop. It featured a faded striped awning. Some of the letters stenciled on the window had begun to peel away.

They stepped into the tiny store. One wall was crammed with fishing gear and the shelves crowded with snorkels, dive masks, wet suits and Scuba equipment. The bald man behind the counter looked up over the top of his half-glasses, putting down the clipboard he'd been poring over.

"Help you folks?"

His eyes were dark, the irises lost in the black pupils.

"I'm a private investigator," Sergio said, giving him a glance at the card in his wallet. "I'm looking into the death of a woman who visited this shop three years ago. What's your name, sir?"

The man looked startled. "Lionel Burnette."

Sergio let that revelation sit untouched for a moment. To her credit, Helen did not react either. "A woman named Fiona Ross came to visit your shop." Sergio showed him a picture of Fiona on his cell phone. "Do you remember her?"

He squinted at the image. "Can't say as I do."

"Can you find out if she purchased anything here?"

He nodded and punched some keys in his computer. "There she is. Fiona Ross. Not a purchase, she reserved some rental equipment."

"What exactly?"

"Snorkel, dive mask, wet suit."

Sergio blinked. His sister really had planned a dive. "When did she return the gear?"

"That's the thing. She never showed up to claim the equipment in the first place. Says here she paid in cash, almost two hundred dollars, and there's a note. 'Customer will be by to pick up gear by 6:00 p.m.'" He peered again over his half-glasses. "She never showed."

Because she was dead. Helen moved subtly, her palm warm on his shoulder.

"Mr. Burnette, we were wondering about a man you might know, possibly a relative. His name is Kyle Burnette."

Lionel's demeanor changed. The amiable expression vanished, shuttered behind hardened eyes. "Kyle's my cousin. What about him?"

Sergio leaned forward. "Does he come here often?"

"Sometimes. Does a little work for me. Why?"

"We want to ask him some questions."

"About what?"

"That's between us and him." Sergio knew his own tone was taut with anger. It was the wrong approach. Lionel drew back.

"He used to be into some stuff, got in trouble for helping move some product he shouldn't have, but he doesn't do that anymore. He's an honest guy."

That was more than Sergio could take. "Then you won't mind giving me his number or address, so I can ask him a few questions?"

"I'll tell him you're looking for him."

"We can get the cops over here," Sergio said.

Lionel's eyes slitted. "Go ahead. I think Kyle's on a trip now, a real long one, and I think he's about to buy a new cell phone with a new number. He might even be moving and I'm sure he won't remember to give me his new address. I'll tell the cops the same thing."

Sergio wanted to reach across the counter and rattle the shop owner's teeth. Helen tugged on Sergio's sleeve. "Thank you for your help. We'll be back if we have more questions."

Sergio fumed, but he followed. "I could have pressed him harder. Why…?"

She whispered in his ear. "I saw Kyle through the window. He's headed toward the alley."

Sergio pushed through the door in time to see Kyle Burnette just about to turn down the narrow passageway between the two buildings.

His mouth went slack with shock when he spotted them, and he took off in a sprint. Sergio bolted down the alley behind him.

Helen reacted a beat slower than Sergio. She snagged her cell phone from her pocket and chased after them.

Burnette stumbled and almost went down, but he kept going, kicking an empty bucket behind him.

Sergio jumped over it and kept up the pursuit. She slowed and went around the obstacle. Should she stop and call the cops? She was afraid to leave the chase in case Sergio needed another set of eyes to track Burnette.

They burst from the alley into the rear parking lot. Sergio lunged out at Burnette and this time he sent him stumbling, but Sergio lost his footing as well, skidding on some gravel. They both went down, tumbling in different directions. Sergio rolled several times, springing to his feet again as Burnette sprang up and disappeared around a row of cars.

"He might have a weapon," Sergio snapped back at Helen. "Go back and call the cops." He took off again around the nearest car. Helen meant to comply, until she heard a shout and a thud. She cleared the first car to find Sergio sprawled face-first across the hood of a car.

SEVENTEEN

Justin Dover, eyes wide, leaped from his car, leaving the door open. He hurried to Sergio who was straightening up. Sergio looked dazed, but she did not see any obvious injuries.

"Are you hurt?" she said.

Sergio shook his head and Justin let out a puff of air.

"That's a relief. I was pulling into the parking lot when Sergio came around the corner, running like his hair was on fire. I could have killed you, man. What gives?"

"Sorry," Sergio said, wiping his scraped palms on his jeans. "I was chasing someone."

Helen fingered the phone. "Do you need an ambulance?"

Sergio waved her off, scanning the parking lot with a look of disgust.

Justin arched a brow. "Who was the guy, by the way, and why are you chasing him? I just got a look at the back of him, I think, before you crashed into my car."

"His name is Kyle Burnette," Helen said. "He's the one who was trying to get into the lodge, and we think he's trying to keep us out of the tunnels."

Justin's look was quizzical. "Why would he care? I thought they were all closed up now."

"We don't know why he's interested yet." Sergio had caught his breath. "I'm going to head to the truck to see if I can track where he went, though he's probably long gone or he's found himself a good hiding place."

Justin nodded. "I'll do the same in my car."

Sergio gave Justin his cell phone number. "Call if you spot him."

"Will do."

Helen saw Lionel peering from the rear shop window. He didn't exactly smile, but he was clearly pleased that his cousin had escaped.

Justin noticed her interest. "The dive-shop guy a friend of yours?" he asked, one hand on the roof of his vehicle.

"Kyle's Burnette's cousin and absolutely no help at all," Sergio snapped.

She sighed. "What are you doing here, Justin? Are you into diving?"

"No way. Not unless you count soaking in a hot tub. I'm returning some fishing poles for Gavin."

Sergio arched a brow. "For Gavin? You're an obliging friend."

Justin shrugged. "Mostly just killing time between sessions at the lodge. Besides, Gavin's got a pregnant wife to tend to. He rented some poles and we were going to try to fish during the conference, but he couldn't make it for some reason." He shrugged. "I'll return the poles later after I make a few rounds searching for Burnette." He climbed in and slammed the door.

Helen saw the top of a fishing pole just visible above the seat in Justin's car as he reversed. She knew Sergio had made note of it too.

They parted ways, Sergio and Helen returning to the

truck and slowly circling the block, widening their search area to no avail. Helen finally got Sergio to stop and pulled a small first-aid kit from her bag. She dabbed at his scraped palms. He winced. The repressed energy in his taut muscles telegraphed his feelings.

Helen sucked in a breath. “Before you ask, Fiona didn’t talk to me about diving, at least not that I can remember. Maybe she figured she’d go without me.”

Color stained his cheeks. “She wouldn’t have planned to go alone unless it was really important. She knew about dive safety.”

“She might have intended to ask someone else to go with her, but she… I mean…she never got the chance.” She tried to apply a bandage to his palm, but he would not allow it. “It’s fine,” he said, “just a scrape,” but he sounded as if his thoughts were far away.

“Sergio,” she said. “Do you think Fiona was going to go down into the tunnels?”

He didn’t answer, just looked out the windshield. “She should have called me, but I was off somewhere, playing around, enjoying my life with no responsibilities.”

“This isn’t your fault.”

His eyes snapped to hers. “Then it isn’t yours either. Can we agree on that?”

She didn’t know how to respond. “I guess… I…” She stopped. “I just can’t help wondering if she didn’t keep the dive plans from me because I was too busy. Too busy to help.”

“You were busy. Let yourself off the hook. The Bible says you’re forgiven, you and me. Are we gonna believe that or not?” There was something sharp-edged in his tone, like a broken shard of glass.

Was she going to believe the words she’d been taught?

The words she so easily reminded others about? Was she forgiven for her sins or wasn't she? She suddenly felt a taste of freedom she had not experienced for three long years, a whisper of peace, an echo of hope.

"Yes," she said finally, eyes filling. "I do believe that."

"Okay," he said. "Then let's start living like it, you and me. What happened to Fiona wasn't my responsibility or yours. We could have, should have, done things differently, but we are not at fault for her death. Agreed?"

Helen nodded, still mystified by the intensity which bubbled from him. "Then why do you sound so angry, Sergio?"

"Because someone out there is at fault, someone who is going to pay. I don't know how and I don't know when, but I will see to it that they do."

Their earlier conversation came back to Helen. She had the feeling the latest setback had put Sergio close to an edge that would not support him, a rickety place where he would risk everything in the name of justice for Fiona.

"The police…" she tried.

"Are inadequate."

"I'm afraid you're going to do something dangerous, Sergio."

He didn't answer, just stared out the window at something she could not see. She touched his shoulder and still he did not move. "Maybe we should stop before this goes too far."

"I will not stop. I can't. I know that now."

"Your girls—what if vengeance takes away their father? Is it worth that price?"

"It won't come to that," he said.

A thrill of fear coursed through her as he cranked

the engine and guided them back on the road. It was as though darkness had settled on him, crowding away everything else. She tried to think of something to fill the dangerous silence.

"Strange that Gavin was set to go fishing and then changed his mind," she said slowly.

"I thought that too. Maybe he's been meeting Burnette at the dive shop and he used the fishing idea as a smokescreen. He sent Justin back to return them so he wouldn't be seen there." He drove back along the main street, taking the road that led away from town.

"Where are we going?" she finally asked.

"I need you to show me."

She already knew what he meant, but she asked the question anyway, dread building inside like rising floodwaters. "Show you what?"

"The place where you and Fiona got out of those tunnels."

"Sergio, that was years ago. I might not be able to find it."

"Then I will." He finally looked at her then. "Helen, I'm going back in those tunnels and I'm going to find out what Burnette and whoever he's working with are so desperate to hide."

She swallowed the lump of fear that clogged her throat. Before she could answer, he fixed her with a look so steely she almost didn't recognize him.

"And I'm doing it alone."

Whatever connection she thought she'd felt between them seemed a faraway figment of her imagination at that moment. He did not want her by his side and she suspected it was not just to shield her from danger. They had embraced the fact that God forgave them, and so they should forgive themselves. What a grand freedom that was, a terrible weight lifted. She'd always be grateful that Sergio forced her to reconcile her faith and her failures, but he was clearly not interested in anything further, deeper.

Alone.

Forcing down an onslaught of sadness and disappointment, she sat back and let him drive them into the flickering shadows of the woods.

Sergio knew he was hurting her by inserting the wall between them. He was hurting himself, probably, shutting off the yearnings of his heart, returning them to cordial friendship and nothing more. Why? The answer was fear, pure and simple. Fear that she'd be hurt in his relentless pursuit of justice, fear that his kindling emotions would turn into something he could not handle. But the greatest fear of all was that he would let her in, allow her to become the central part of his life and soul, the part where the girls now lived, and then he'd lose her. Their relationship might end for any number of reasons: the past might choke out the present, she might not want to take on two toddlers. There could be an accident, an illness, a million things that could break either one of them.

People died, unions ended. If he was alone, he might have the courage to risk it, but now he had to give one-hundred-percent of himself to his girls because he could not allow them to lose anyone else. So there it was, the terrible irony. Fear would prevent him from reaching out to Helen, but it also fueled his desire for revenge.

There was only one avenue open to him. He must ensure that things turned out so he'd never have to look his little girls in the eyes and tell them he'd failed to find their mother's murderer. He could not walk away as Helen had asked him to. Laurel and Lucy had to be his first priority and securing their future meant he had to make choices. Difficult, soul-searing choices.

They drove slowly along a narrow, two-lane road that was cracked and hemmed in by tall grasses.

"This is the road you hiked back to meet Gavin and Justin?"

"Yes. We exited the tunnels and walked west. I'm sure because we were facing the direction of the ocean. It wasn't a proper exit, just a hole, really, a place where the tunnel wall had failed and somebody, kids or maybe the guys using the tunnels for transporting drugs, had scooped away the debris."

They got out of the truck and hiked both sides of the road until they were tired and their pants speckled with mud. "Maybe I was wrong," she mused.

Justin texted to let them know he had not seen any sign of Kyle Burnette, which didn't surprise Sergio. The guy was holed up somewhere. He was a local and knew every crack and crevice in which to lay low, maybe even in the dive shop itself, with his loyal cousin Lionel. Biting back his frustration, he wiped his forehead, hands still stinging from his close encounter with the parking lot pavement. "I'll come back alone later," he said. "I don't want to keep you out here too long in case Burnette has regrouped and saw us leave town."

Helen's forehead furrowed. "It all looks so different after all these years, so overgrown and…" She broke off. "There," she said, pointing to a towering pile of granite, dotted with shrubs that poked from the cracks. "The stallion."

"What stallion?"

Helen stared up at the mass of rocks. "It was late when we made our way out, but there was some moonlight. We were giddy with relief that we'd found an escape. We were getting scared, though we'd never have admitted it to the boys for anything. When we crawled out, Fiona announced that this clump of rocks looked just like a stallion." She pointed. "That narrow dark-colored streak? That's where the mane is. Can you see it?"

He couldn't, but Fiona had and that was all that mattered. He breathed through a sudden pain in his chest as he thought of her, a young girl with a whole life to live. "Fiona was always obsessed with horses." It felt so strange to listen to Helen relive the moment from their high school days. He suddenly recalled Fiona's collection of horse figurines, probably still tucked away at his parents' house. He resolved to find those figurines and give them to Lucy and Laurel, and when he did so, he'd tell them all about their mother and her deep love of all things equine. He realized she was looking at him.

"I'm sorry. Does it hurt you to talk about her?" she said.

"Yes, but it's a good pain, to be reminded of the things she loved."

"I understand," she said. She started to reach for his hand but then stopped and he grieved even more the choice he'd made to go it alone. "The opening must be close," she said, picking her way carefully along in the damp weeds that grew at the base of the rock pile.

Another fifteen minutes passed, and he was about to call off the search when he noticed a cool breeze wafting against his ankles. He bent closer. Almost completely concealed by the tall grass was an opening no more than two feet across.

He grabbed a flashlight from his back pocket and bent away the grass, flicking on the beam. The light was swallowed up by the darkness, but he could make out enough to realize the opening led to a passage that sloped down and away from the road.

"I'm going to poke my head in."

Helen nodded and turned on her phone flashlight to add her own meager beam. He slithered into the opening, climbing down a chute which was littered with fallen rock and dried pine needles. The scent of earth and damp assailed him. In the shadows something small skittered away, probably a rat which he sincerely hoped did not return. It was part of the reason he loved oceans…no rodents.

He took a couple of steps forward, bent nearly double, his elbows scraping the dirt on either side. Gradually the passageway widened and the earthen floor gave way to a path of stone that trailed into the darkness. He wanted to press on right then and there, to plunge into the gloom until he had some answers, but he was unwilling to leave Helen for too long. Before he turned back, he picked up a rock and tossed it as far as he could down the dark gullet of the tunnel. He heard what he'd expected, a dull splash. Was this where Fiona had intended to explore with the dive gear? More questions to taunt him.

Don't worry, sis. I won't give up until I find what you were looking for.

EIGHTEEN

Helen heaved a breath when Sergio emerged, brushing dirt off his shoulders and the knees of his jeans. "I'll go rent some dive gear in another town. No way I'm trusting Lionel to provide my equipment," Sergio was saying. "Plus he'd probably be on the phone to his cousin before I even left the shop."

Her nerves were still rattled. She began to wonder if maybe she shouldn't have helped Sergio find the second entrance. An air of something sinister permeated that long-forgotten place and she could not rid her mind of the fear that the tunnels would claim another life. There was no hope that she would talk him out of it, though. She was trying to figure out a way to ensure he would at least take Mitch and Chad with him, when her phone buzzed.

"Hi, Liam," she said as her brother's voice charged through the line. "I'm with Sergio. We were following a lead, but…it didn't pan out, not yet." She rolled her eyes as he launched in. "Don't start, please. I'm perfectly safe, I promise." She covered the phone. "He's finally got a flight out tomorrow morning."

Sergio sighed in relief, she thought, which pained her. She could imagine what he was thinking. Big brother would be back on his home turf, keeping a watchful eye out on Helen. She'd be safe, out of his hair, and he'd be free to dive the tunnels until he found what he was looking for. What if he dove into that terrible, dismal place and did not come out alive? Her stomach clenched.

Something Liam said poked through her daze and she jolted, pressing the phone to her ear. "What did you say?" He repeated, and her spirit leaped. "Of course," she said. "How could I have forgotten that? I'll go look right now."

"I don't want you to…" her brother started.

She forged ahead quickly before Liam had a chance to work up a proper tirade. "I won't do it alone," she said. "I will make sure I've got a full squad of brothers along with me when I search. I'm glad you're coming home. I've missed you and I want to hear all about your trip." She disconnected and smiled at what she'd heard from Liam.

"What?" Sergio said. "You're grinning like a Cheshire cat."

"Did I mention my brother has a near-perfect memory?"

"No, but I'm not surprised. I'm beginning to think there's nothing he's not good at."

"Cooking. He's a terrible cook."

"I feel his pain. In spite of my fetching apron, I'm a complete failure in the kitchen."

"I texted him about the memory book and he just reminded me that we had a problem with mice in the lodge basement shortly after I took over. We packed everything up and moved it while the pest guys did their work, but we ran short on space so some of my personal items were taken to the old barn. We intended to move them back, but it slipped off the radar." Excitement prickled her spine and she could tell Sergio felt the same.

"The old barn in the back? The girls and I took a walk out there."

She nodded. "We've built a new one, so that building is used for storage now."

"That means your belongings are still there, safe and sound?"

She lifted her shoulders. "One can only hope." She paused, suddenly uncertain. "Do you…want to look with me?"

"Absolutely," he said. "But you'd better alert your brother squad, like you promised Liam."

She started sending texts to Mitch and Chad. Maybe it was all for the best. The more brothers around, the less alone time with Sergio.

Trying to summon a sense of peace, she could only hope that at long last they'd find the memory book that Fiona had been looking for and it would reveal the answers they so desperately sought.

She was surprised to find that it was after six when they finally arrived back at the lodge. Waiters in plaid shirts and black jeans flitted back and forth past the dining room windows, carrying pans of pasta and steamed green beans with bacon to place on the buffet tables. She'd mentally revisited the algorithm she'd used to calculate the amounts of cherry cobbler and vanilla ice cream. Hopefully, she'd been spot-on.

"I have to see to the dinner service," she said ruefully. "Can we start our search after that?"

"Sure. Gives me time to eat with the girls before Mitch and Chad get here."

"Why don't I have something sent over for you?"

"No, thanks," he said. "I can make dinner for them."

"It's no trouble, really."

His eyes flashed. “Helen, I can take care of my children.”

She stepped back. “Of course. I didn’t mean to imply you couldn’t.”

He hung his head and blew out a breath. “I’m sorry. I know you didn’t. That was rude and ungrateful of me. I’m tired and amped up and feeling guilty because I haven’t been there with the girls.” He gave her a lopsided grin. “The reality is, Betty deserves to have a meal prepared for her. It would be nice, if you would have something sent over. I, we all, would appreciate it.”

“Great. I’ll ask Tiny right now.”

“Thank you.”

Helen felt suddenly better, lighter. Everything was spiraling out of control, dead end after dead end, one dangerous encounter crowded in on the heels of the next, but there was dinner to provide. It was a small thing to do, arranging some pasta and cherry cobbler for Sergio and his little family, but at least she could make sure the girls had a nice meal. Fiona would be pleased, and that thought made her smile. It was an entirely new feeling to think about Fiona without the accompanying guilt, she realized, as she headed to the kitchen. She would always be grateful to Sergio for helping release her from that burden. She wished she had a gift to give him in return.

Hopefully, the memory book would be found and clues uncovered that would render it unnecessary for Sergio to go down into those tunnels.

She resolved to do everything in her power to make that happen.

Sergio took another shower, changed his clothes and boots and quickly looked up the name of a nearby dive shop before he said hello to the girls. They wanted to show him the animals they'd cut from construction paper. He was grateful when Betty clued him in.

"I'm sure Daddy loves your paper horsies," she said.

"Oh, yes. For sure," Sergio said. "Those are really amazing horsies."

Betty gathered up the mangled pieces. "I'll put these on the fridge. I think I have some magnets in my bag."

Mary Poppins could not possibly have a more well-supplied bag than Betty. He heard Helen knock a few minutes later. He left the girls with directions to tidy up and opened the door to find her in fresh jeans and a flowered cotton shirt, holding a container full of spaghetti and garlic bread. The scent made his mouth water.

"My taste buds are fixin' to have a hoedown," he said.

"I'll tell Tiny. He'll be very gratified, I'm sure."

He was just about to thank her when a shrill scream split the air.

He launched himself down the hall, arriving in the girls' room to find Laurel red-faced, her mouth opened wide in midscream. Lucy stood near the dresser with Laurel's purple rabbit in her hands and a pair of scissors in the other. The bunny's severed ear lay on the floor.

He gaped in disbelief as he took in Lucy's chagrin. "What happened? Did you cut Bunny's ear off?"

Lucy dropped her head and would not meet his gaze as he took the scissors from her. "These are only for craft time," he said sternly. "That's the rule. You know that." He could barely make himself heard over her caterwauling sister.

Laurel's shrieking rose to ear-rupturing decibels until a vein started pulsing in his temple. He was desperate to stop the noise.

"Laurel, I'll fix it, okay, honey?" He had precisely

zero knowledge of needle and thread, but Betty was a quilter and he figured she could whip something else out of her cavernous bag and make everything all right again.

Laurel continued to wail and then to his shock, she grabbed a decorative dish from the table and readied an overhand lob.

"Don't you throw that," he ordered.

But to his utter disbelief, she loosed the missile anyway and it sailed across the room too low for him to snag. It smashed against the wall into dozens of shards. For a moment he was too dumbfounded to do anything. What was happening to his precious girls?

As the dish exploded, Lucy screamed and bolted for the door. Acting on reflex, he intercepted, grabbing her around the waist as Laurel leaped at her sister, clutching a handful of her hair.

"Stop it," he thundered to no avail.

Laurel yanked Lucy's hair as she dangled in the crook of Sergio's arm, causing Lucy to yelp like an agitated puppy. He danced in an awkward attempt to separate the sisters.

Betty trotted through the door, Helen just behind her. Immediately, Betty hurried over and pried Laurel's fingers from Lucy's hair until the two were disconnected, with Lucy settling into a whimpering bundle. She gathered Laurel up on her hip.

"I'll put Laurel on a time-out in my room and you can do the same with Lucy in here," Betty said, marching away with the still wailing child.

He stood there, breathing hard, Lucy motionless at his feet. "What just happened?"

"I'll get a broom and sweep up the glass," Helen said.

While she was gone he tried to pull himself together. Betty had said Laurel was on a time-out so he grabbed on to that lifeline. "Lucy," he said, lifting her boneless body from the floor and carrying her to the sofa, "you're going to sit here for five minutes and think of how to say you're sorry to your sister for cutting Bunny's ear. Do you understand?"

Lucy stared stonily at him, her mouth pinched into a tiny hostile circle.

"Do you understand that you have to say you're sorry, Lucy?" he repeated slowly.

Finally Lucy bobbed her head once, face blotched from crying, and huddled into a ball on the cushions. He was torn. Should he go to her? Offer comfort? She looked so miserable. But she had done wrong, and Betty seemed to think time-outs were in order. Limits were important, he'd read. Rules were to be followed and Lucy had to understand he meant it if he was going to succeed long-term at this parenting thing. *Right?* Feeling torn in two, he stood there helplessly.

Helen whisked the glass into a dustpan and he followed her to the kitchen. Betty joined them.

"Everyone to their corners," she said as Sergio handed her the bunny and the severed ear.

"Can you?" he pleaded, wondering how he'd been reduced to begging.

"I can reattach, but he's never going to win any bunny beauty pageants. I've got a sewing kit in my bag. Give me a few minutes."

She left, and Sergio sank down into a chair with a groan.

Helen sat next to him. "It's a hard job, being a parent."

His insides were still twisted in knots. "They're usually so sweet. Is this kind of thing going to happen a lot in the future?"

Helen smiled. "I don't have a sister, but I know plenty of people who do, and they say the fighting is pretty normal."

"That was normal? It was like a mixed-martial-arts match with no rules." He forced out a breath. "I hate to think what their fights will look like when they're sixteen."

Inside, he battled the desperate feelings that shamed him, the reminders of how free he used to be, how much he missed diving, the adventure, the travel, the rush. Now he was in deeper waters than he'd ever been, and the responsibility was crushing. The weight of it tumbled from his mouth. "I miss my old life." Heat flooded his cheeks at the admission, especially in front of Helen. "I love those girls one-hundred-percent, but I mourn what I've lost." He did not see condemnation in her eyes, disgust on her face. "That's wrong, I know."

She reached out and covered his hand with hers. "Not wrong. That's honest. You're entitled to feel that way. I think anybody would, especially in your situation."

He was so grateful for her understanding that he pulled her hand to his mouth and grazed his lips over her smooth skin, allowing himself to rest there for a moment, to find peace in their connection. Then he remembered what he'd decided, that he would go it alone, him and the girls.

But when he laid his head on the table, she stroked his hair and it was like the warm shallow waters of Palau, his last dive before Fiona died, the dancing of light off the waves flickering through his memory. He'd felt that God was speaking to him in those deep waters, showing him a tiny glimpse of how exquisite life could be. But he'd been alone then, with no one to share it. And now, he was dodging flying objects, issuing time-outs and living caught between guilt and inexpressible love for his girls.

He spoke, his words muffled by the tabletop. "Sometimes, I have no idea what to do and when the spaghetti is flying everywhere there just isn't time to consult a parenting book or read a blog. I make the wrong decisions more often than the right ones."

She got up from the table and hugged him from behind, her cheek close to his. "Lucy and Laurel know you love them. They know it when you're having fun together, and they know it when you're disciplining them. That is what good parenting looks like."

Good parenting? He wasn't so sure, but in that instant he desperately wanted to bring Helen close, to lay out his insecurities and faults and failures that had built up inside him like nitrogen bubbles from decompressing a dive too quickly.

She was Fiona's best friend. That notion strummed discordant notes through his soul. *The one you kept far away from the girls until a few days ago.* It only added another heap to his pile of bad decisions and guilt. He'd been wrong to blame Helen, but he'd also be wrong to let things go any further between them.

Remember your number-one job—find Fiona's killer and raise your girls. Both those endeavors would require his whole life, his entire being and there was not enough left over to share with a woman, especially not Helen. If he didn't risk loving, he'd never have to risk losing.

He mused for a moment, imagining what their lives could have been like if she wasn't Fiona's friend, if his sister had never gone down in those tunnels that terrible night. Maybe he would have met Helen somehow, they'd have fallen in love and built a family of their own.

A pang of pain ripped through him. As beautiful as that image was, he would not trade the painful and poignant experience of being father to Laurel and Lucy. His path was fixed, and it would ultimately take him away from Helen.

It took every ounce of strength to separate himself from her, but he cleared his throat and smiled. "Thanks, Helen. Let's see if the two wrestling champs are ready for some dinner."

NINETEEN

Helen stayed at Sergio's request while the girls ate. He glanced back and forth at them as if they were a pair of wild animals, but they were soon eating and giggling normally after Lucy apologized to her sister and gave her a tight hug. Betty produced the repaired bunny rabbit and order had been restored, at least temporarily. The little domestic scene tugged at Helen's heartstrings, but her nerves were buzzing with excitement at the prospect of locating the memory book. If it could possibly contain the clue to Trish's and Fiona's murders, she intended to find it, especially if it would keep Sergio out of danger and home for moments like these with his girls.

With dinner finished and the dishes put away, Helen and Sergio left the cabin and joined Mitch and Chad. Both brothers were sitting on the low stone retaining wall watching the cabin. She felt her cheeks warm to think of them out there doing sentry duty while she ate with Sergio and the girls. Why hadn't they knocked on the door?

"You could have come in," she said.

Mitch didn't smile; he rarely did unless his wife or little boy was around, but she thought his lip crimped in amusement.

"No sense interrupting your dinner date."

Date? Cheeks flaming, she was about to retort that it was no such thing, but he'd already started off in the direction of the old barn, Chad next to him. She would have to tell Mitch in no uncertain terms that there would be no dates between her and Sergio, no further contact at all except to help him find Fiona's killer. That's all Fiona would have wanted anyway, wasn't it? She allowed herself a moment to consider the question swirling through her mind. What would Fiona, her best friend, think about the deep feelings she was developing for Sergio?

She thought about what kind of woman Fiona had grown into, widowed at such an early age. Yes, she'd grown more sedate; the old Fiona was always ready for fun and even mischief, but there was a solid, quiet strength about the grown-up Fiona when she spoke of her daughters. The teen she'd known had turned into a woman who wanted the best for her kids, but who also cared about people enough to want to solve the mystery of what happened to Trish. How easily she could have dismissed her suspicions, ended her visit and gone back to her babies, her world, but she had not. She'd taken a risk for Trish, for a friendship violently ended, unsuspecting that she would give up her own life in the process.

Poor Lucy and Laurel. Helen thought about the temper tantrum she'd witnessed, as well as happier moments like the mud-puddle fishing and crayon coloring. They had a birthday coming up and she meant to suggest to Sergio that she would be happy to host a party at the lodge for them.

A shiver of uncertainty went through her. Fiona would approve of her boldly attempting to solve the murder, and even helping Sergio in his duties as a father, but certainly she wouldn't want Helen assuming any more of a role in her family than that. Would she? Godmother was one thing, an honorary title, but arranging birthday parties and helping Sergio navigate day-to-day tantrums? *It doesn't matter anyway*, she told herself. They'd be gone soon.

"You okay?" Sergio said, touching her arm.

"Oh, yes," she said. She wasn't about to tell him of her angst. She had to stay focused, in spite of the fact that her emotions were an unpredictable cascade when he was around. *Fiona died looking for answers. Don't let the same thing happen to Sergio.*

She suddenly emerged from her mental funk to realize what was missing. "Mitch, where's Jingles?"

"Aunt Ginny snagged him for a bath. She says we can't have a dog smelling up the lodge."

"Uh-oh. How did Jingles take that?" Helen said.

"He was howling like she was fixing to remove his spleen or something. Took Uncle Gus and Stew to catch him. I'll go to the ranch after we're done and rescue him," Mitch said as he flipped on the lights in the old barn. They'd used it for some ranch-style hoedowns upon occasion before the new barn had been built. The lower level was crowded with stacked chairs, some hedge trimmers and rakes and a pile of old saddles that had fallen into disrepair. The smell of hay permeated the place even after decades of disuse. A wooden ladder led to the open loft level. The scant light did not quite drive away the early-evening shadows from the far recesses of the space. Her pulse quickened at the sight of the plastic containers stacked with tidy precision in the loft before they'd been forgotten.

Mitch went up first. "All clear. Come on up."

The three remaining climbed up the ladder. "I'll take the plastic bins," she said. "You two can search the boxes." Helen had to put her embarrassment aside as the men began to paw through her possessions. An assortment of high school yearbooks elicited some laughter from the guys. In another box were various certificates and a few trophies, mementos of her academic pursuits. Top of her class, near-perfect scores on college entrance exams. What did it all mean now? Less than nothing.

"We always knew you were smart," Chad said, holding up a medallion fastened to a ribbon. "Now we've got proof."

"Smart enough to know better, that's what my dad always used to say." She felt the dull ache she always experienced when she thought of her father. Back in the days immediately following her mother's death, he'd tried to be an interested parent, but he could not defeat the mountain of despair. More recently he'd attempted to make contact. She'd reached back in turn, eager to resurrect the love she'd felt for him, but Liam had never wanted to bridge the gap, until very recently when she'd detected a thawing in his anger. Helen smiled. Maggie was the perfect match for Liam, a woman who encouraged him in all the ways he needed.

Opening a plastic bin, Helen found yet another stuffed bear, this one Liam had given her for graduation. It was because of her big brother that she'd actually made it through high school. Setting it aside, she fished out a plastic bag. Her breathing shallowed. She reached in with shaking hands and pulled out the small memory book with the pink leather cover. Even without reading the neatly inked title she knew what it would say.

Remembering Trish.

Incredible. After all the searching, here it was. She must have made some kind of startled noise, because all three men moved closer.

Sergio peered at what she held; a tentative grin broke across his face like a sun rising over the beach and it lit something inside her too. "Is it...?"

She nodded, clutching it to her chest.

"Yes, this is the book Fiona made for us. It was here in the loft the whole time." Sergio overturned the bin for her to sit on and she opened it and flipped through the pages.

The photos had dimmed with time, but they were still clear enough. Going back to the beginning, she scanned the first one. Her stomach knotted when she realized the situation. It was a picture of the five of them crowded into a booth at the local diner. The boys each clutched a huge burger, making faces to the camera. Trish and Fiona sat with her on the other side, heads together, holding up milkshakes. "We stopped for a meal that night," Helen forced out.

"Who took the photo?" Mitch asked.

"A waitress." Her voice cracked, her mind traveling back in time as she relived the scene. "It was taken before we went into those tunnels." Those horrible tunnels, those perilous hours she desperately wished she could get back. Everything about the group in the picture emanated youth and playfulness, an innocence that sparked them with life.

Gavin, the dark-haired jokester who could talk football for hours. Justin, the flashy dresser who loved fishing and worked two jobs. Trish, a social butterfly eager at the prospect of going away to college; Fiona, sensitive, older than her years, a punster. And Helen herself, academically driven, a pleaser, ridiculously happy to be included in the harebrained outing. None of them had the vaguest notion that within hours, their lives would change forever. She realized she was shaking.

"Let's take it back to the lodge," Mitch suggested. "Find a private place and scrutinize it properly."

"How about I save you the trouble?"

They all jerked toward the voice. Kyle Burnette's head popped up as he climbed another rung on the ladder until his torso came into view. Helen's throat closed up in terror as she spotted the gun in his hands, aimed straight at her heart.

"Hand it over," he said with a grin.

Teeth clenched, Sergio berated himself for not hearing Burnette's approach. He could tell Mitch and Chad were doing the same. They'd all been so focused on the photo book. Burnette had probably gotten in just behind them and hidden amongst the equipment on the lower level. How had he known they'd be looking in the old barn? Good old-fashioned surveillance, Sergio figured. He'd likely snuck onto lodge property again and been watching.

"There's nothing in these photos," Sergio growled. He edged a step closer, but Burnette waved the gun at him.

"Don't. I can't miss at this range. Hand me the book."

Helen clutched the volume to her chest. "It's just some high school pictures. Why do you want it?"

"I'm being paid to want it." He waggled the gun. "Now."

Sergio saw Chad slowly raising his arm and he realized he was holding an old trophy. He was going to launch it at Burnette. But what if Burnette got off a shot first? Sergio had to make sure Helen was not in the line of fire.

"Who are you working for?" Mitch snapped.

Burnette didn't move, but his attention was drawn, just as Mitch had no doubt intended. Sergio shuffled forward another few inches, now level with Helen's shoulder.

"I'm not here to talk. The book," Burnette ordered. "'Cuz bullets hurt, in case you aren't clear on that point." He fingered the trigger and stared at Sergio. "If you take another step I'll shoot her." Sergio felt a river of pure unadulterated rage gush through him like a riptide, tugging his good sense away.

"That is the last thing you want to do." His tone was so guttural, he did not recognize his own voice. Chad had now raised the trophy up enough to manage a throw. As he let it loose, Sergio dove in front of Helen, knocking her to the floor.

The trophy sailed over Burnette's head and he fired the gun, the bullet burying itself into a wooden beam behind them. He'd readjusted to shoot again when there was a sound of movement below. Sergio could not see who it was.

Burnette jerked a look around, losing his hold on the ladder. With a startled cry he plummeted backward. Sergio scrambled away from Helen and peered down below, Mitch and Chad right after him.

Gavin and Justin were staring at Burnette's body, splayed awkward and still on top of a wooden pallet.

TWENTY

"He has a gun," Mitch shouted down, but Sergio did not figure Burnette was in any shape to use it. Mitch and Chad descended the ladder and he turned back to Helen, who was on her feet now, photo book still clutched to her body, mouth slack with horror.

"Are you okay?" he said.

She nodded, and forgetting his earlier resolve, he pressed her close, brushing his lips to her temple, smoothing her hair. "Thank God for that." He meant every word, he realized in that moment. He could withstand the heartache of losing Fiona, the angst of parental failure and the loss of his career, but he would not be able to shoulder the sorrow that would ruin him if Helen was killed.

Is it worth it? This dangerous mission you're on? Is it worth risking your life and Helen's? Would the taste of revenge satisfy him if the unthinkable happened? He pushed the thoughts from his mind and buried his face in the sweet scent of her hair and held her close, their erratic breathing mingling until Mitch called up from below.

"Ambulance is rolling. It's secure down here."

Helen tensed and looked at Sergio, lips still pinched in fear. "Is he…?"

"Not sure. We'll find out."

She gave him a brave nod as they peered down below. Chad was kneeling next to Burnette. It looked as though Mitch had found the gun and eased it away with his boot.

He felt her trembling as he took her hand. "Let's get you down from this loft before the police arrive."

She nodded and he guided her toward the ladder. "I'll go first. You sure you're okay to do this now?"

She sucked in a breath and tucked the photo book into her waistband to free up her hands for the descent. "I'll be a lot better if these pictures will bring this to an end."

"I'll second that." Sergio climbed down, keeping an eye on Helen to be sure she was steady as she took the rungs.

"What is going on?" Gavin said. His gelled hair gleamed in the electric light. "Why were you up there? What happened?"

Justin's startled gaze wandered from the fallen Burnette to the book Helen was pulling from her waistband. "Allyson told us you asked about a photo book Fiona made back in high school. Is that it?"

Helen nodded and all of them looked at Burnette, who was breathing, eyes closed as the distant wail of a siren split the air.

"And this guy was out to get it too," Gavin said, more a statement than a question. "I wonder why."

"Why are you two here?" Sergio said, cutting off her answer.

"We saw you all walking this way and we were curious about what you were doing," Gavin said. "Allyson told us you were trying to search the tunnels. We wanted to help end this thing."

"Help?" Sergio didn't bother to keep the doubt from his voice.

Gavin's hands went to his hips. "Yeah, help."

"Do you know this guy?" Sergio said, pointing to Burnette.

Justin shook his head.

Gavin frowned. "Why would I?"

Sergio discounted Gavin's look of confusion, which might be pure artifice. "He hangs out at the dive shop where you rented the fishing poles."

"So because I happen to rent fishing poles from the only dive shop in town you suspect me of being in collusion with him?" Gavin gestured to Burnette.

"Easy now," Justin said. "He didn't mean anything by it."

"Yes, he did," Gavin spat, dark color staining his cheeks. "Same old same old since we were in high school. I've had enough of being accused. A girl dies fifteen years ago, and I'm a suspect now too?"

Justin held up a hand but Gavin's face contorted in anger.

"I wanted to help, but I see that was a mistake. I'm going back to the lodge. My wife told me not to come to Driftwood for this conference, and she was right. I'll always be seen as a criminal here." He shot a look at Justin. "We both will no matter how much time passes." He stalked out of the barn as two medics jogged in. Evonne ran in on their heels. She clasped Helen around the shoulders and the two women stepped into the shadows as the medics began to work on Burnette.

Justin rubbed his eyes. "Don't be too hard on Gavin. He's tied in knots about his wife giving birth. It's all starting to hit home, I think. There are..." He cleared his throat and winced. "Some money issues. He's had to sell a parcel of land. Ranching's a money pit." He jutted his chin at Mitch and Chad. "You fellas know that first-hand. Even harder on the smaller operations."

"No doubt about that." Chad edged back to let the paramedics work, his attention swiveling between Burnette and Helen who rejoined them as Evonne left. "I asked her to announce to the guests there's been an accident and to stay inside the lodge." She frowned. "Gavin left?"

"He needs some space." Justin watched the medics load Burnette onto a stretcher. "Is he going to make it?"

The medic adjusted the straps. "We'll transport him quick as we can. Hospital can update you."

Farraday entered, looking guarded, Sergio thought. Mitch brought him up to speed.

"The memory book," Farraday said. "Anything in there of use?"

Helen sighed. "Burnette showed up before I had a chance to look through it thoroughly."

Farraday pursed his lips and blew out a breath. "And you won't, until I've finished with it." There was a satisfied edge to his tone which prickled Sergio's nerves. "I'll be taking it."

Sergio gaped. "She has a right to look through it, Farraday. It's her property."

"No," he said, every syllable clipped. "It's evidence at a crime scene."

"You could give her a few minutes." Mitch's anger blazed across his face.

Farraday smiled, but there was no humor in it. "I don't think so. You've been hounding me, implying I haven't taken the new info on the Fiona Ross murder seriously, practically accusing me of botching the Trish O'Brian case…"

"You did botch it." Sergio could not keep the simmering ire in check any longer. "We've seen the case files. No pictures, a paltry excuse for a written report. We all know…"

Mitch's warning look cut through his tirade, but Farraday was already flush-cheeked with anger, his breaths coming in spurts through his nose. "All right then. In light of your concern about my procedures, this time, I'll make sure to dot the i's and cross the t's. I'll start by taking that memory book, since it seems like Burnette was so hot to get his hands on it, and you're all going to get out of here right now so we can photograph every square inch of this crime scene."

"Chief Farraday, we're not trying to make you look bad…" Helen started.

"Oh, yeah? Well you know what? You did. When you went to Danny Patron over my head and got permission to get into those tunnels, that didn't exactly cement my reputation as a crime fighter." He crooked a finger. "The photo book. Now."

Helen grimaced. "I sent it with Evonne. It's in the lodge."

"Call her," he said, spittle collecting at the corner of his mouth.

Helen pulled out her cell phone and spoke to Evonne. They waited in strained silence until she arrived with the album and a look of puzzlement. Farraday took it without comment.

"Perfect," he said, nodding to another officer who began to photograph the barn. "All of you get out. Wait outside for us to take your statements." A flicker twisted his mouth. "We'll try to get to you as soon as we can, but all this meticulous police work takes a lot of time."

Fury crackled in Sergio's gut as they filed outside. It was dusk, the sky backlit behind streaks of copper clouds. Evonne returned to her duties.

Another police car arrived with two officers aboard and Sergio was separated from the others and asked for his statement. It seemed like hours passed before they were allowed to return to the barn. They gathered at a table in the empty reception room for cups of coffee.

None of them talked much. There had been no word from the hospital until Danny Patron called and Mitch put him on speakerphone.

"You've gotten yourselves into another mess," he said.

"'Fraid so. And we've angered Farraday."

"Embarrassed him, so I'm not surprised." Danny paused. "My daughter is doing great, but I can't return for another few weeks, until she's stronger."

Sergio figured it must be hard for a cop to hand his town over to another, but worrying about that had to take second to his concern for his daughter's health. "I'm pleased to hear she's improving," Sergio said.

He sighed. "Me too. We've been on our knees praying until we've worn out our pant legs, but at long last it looks like she's going to make it."

Helen sighed. "That's the best news I've heard in a long time, Danny."

Patron hesitated. "I'm afraid I've got some that's not so good."

Sergio braced himself.

"I checked with the hospital," he said. "Burnette is in a coma. No telling when and if he's going to pull out of it."

Sergio felt like howling.

"Sorry to end on that note, but I've gotta go."

They thanked him, and Mitch disconnected.

"We are no closer to finding out who Burnette was working for," Sergio groaned. "And now we've lost the memory book too."

"Not exactly."

They all stared at Helen.

"What do you mean, *not exactly*?" Sergio said.

"We don't have the original." Helen toyed with the slender chain around her neck. "I just had a feeling when I sent the book with Evonne that something might happen to it, with all the things that have gone on around here."

"Helen," Sergio said slowly, "what did you do?"

"I asked Evonne to scan the photos and put them in the safe."

It was all he could do not to sweep her up in an exuberant bear hug. "You are a genius," he said.

She blushed. "Some people would not describe my obsessive tendencies quite so nicely."

Sergio stood and offered her his hand. "Don't you think it's about time to look through those photos?"

"Past time, I'd say."

Hope stirred his pulse, or maybe it was the feel of her hand in his as they hurried toward the front desk.

TWENTY-ONE

Helen spread the papers out on the table. The scanned photos were clear, and she was glad she'd invested in a top-of-the-line machine that did the job so well. Mitch, Chad and Sergio arranged themselves at the table, taking the pages one by one after she'd scrutinized them.

Evonne even brought a magnifying glass. The diner photo was first in the album, followed by some close-ups of the girls making faces at the camera. Fiona had not included any other shots of that night. The rest were of the funeral, the guests, the beautiful eight-by-ten of Trish displayed on an easel, the dozens of flower arrangements. What followed were some older snapshots of their high school days. Trish in her cheer outfit, Fiona dressed as the school mascot in a lumpy bear costume, side hugging Gavin in his football gear. One image showed Justin displaying a tiny fish on a hook, Gavin standing next to him, giving him a goofy thumbs down. The last shot was a family photo which she had no idea how Fiona had gotten hold of. Trish and her sister stood on either side of their parents. They were perhaps ten and fourteen at the time, Allyson sporting braces and Trish had the put-upon look of adolescence.

She pored over each photo before passing them on to

the men. They kept at it until their necks ached and her eyes were burning. What could Fiona have seen in the pictures that proved to be her death sentence?

"The back?" Mitch suggested. "Maybe something's written on the flip side of the photos?"

"I hadn't thought of that." Helen felt a surge of excitement and quickly summoned Evonne.

"Sorry," she said. "I took them all out of the plastic sleeves when I scanned them, and there was nothing on the backs."

Helen sighed. Another dead end. She kept circling back to the first photo, the one of them in the diner right before their tunnel excursion. There had to be something she was missing, a tiny clue that detail-oriented Fiona had picked up on.

Her head began to throb, and no answers came.

"I'm sorry," she finally said when the old grandfather clock in the lobby chimed eight. "I'll keep looking, but you don't all have to stay and watch me."

Sergio sat back and she read the disappointment in his expression. "That's enough for now anyway. It's been a long day. Maybe something will occur to you after some sleep."

But he didn't sound hopeful as she gathered up the pages. Mitch went to get Jingles and Chad waited for her to go upstairs.

"I just need some fresh air," she said to Chad.

When he started to argue she touched him gently on the arm. "Just to the front porch."

"And I'll go with her," Sergio said.

Chad looked as if he was still going to fuss, but instead he checked the time. "Okay. A short trip outside won't hurt. If you're not inside in fifteen, I'm coming to find you."

"Yes, warden," she said, teasing.

He didn't reply so she kissed him good night and stepped out onto the porch.

"Little brother is on duty," Sergio said with a tired laugh. "How much longer until Liam arrives to join forces?"

"He lands tomorrow, I think."

Sergio nodded. "Good. The more brothers, the safer you are."

Thinking of the attack in her room, along with the crash on the cliffs, she wondered if she would ever be safe again. Whoever was paying Burnette was still roaming free.

But she was not going to give up, because she had a frightening feeling that Sergio was about to try one more risky undertaking in the tunnels.

And she had to find a way to stop him.

Sergio tried not to let his massive disappointment show. He allowed the chill evening air to revive him, scented with eucalyptus and the aroma of the coffee perking in the lobby. Across the way he saw Betty walk by the cabin window, probably getting the girls ready for bed. It hit him like a brick to the face how close Betty and the girls were to the place where Burnette had fired his weapon. For a moment, he could hardly get a breath. It was awful enough that Helen had stared down the barrel of a gun, but what if a stray bullet had found its way to the girls… He shut down the thought that made his blood run cold. No more, he decided then and there.

Helen sniffed, smothered a small gulp, and he realized she was fighting tears. He pulled her into the circle of his arms, as much to soothe himself as to comfort her. No one had been hurt except Burnette, but the "could haves" weakened his knees.

His embrace tightened and as she tipped her face to his, it was suddenly too much. Their mouths met in a kiss that wrapped him in a cloud of bliss. Again, he floated in that sensation of peaceful tropical seas. He deepened the kiss, although his brain told him in no uncertain terms he was acting a fool. But her arms circled his neck, her sweet fragrance crowding out his saner self if only for a moment. The lingering kiss, one more second of wonder, and then he released her, setting her back carefully, restoring them both to some level of composure. Still he kept his arms around her, not willing yet to let her go completely.

"I…that felt…" she groped for words, "like a goodbye kiss."

He rested his forehead against hers, breathing a little unsteadily. "I shouldn't have allowed this to get out of hand." He shook his head, straightened and restarted. "I mean your brothers were right when they said I was stirring up trouble. I went bullheaded into this thing, without a thought of how it would increase the danger to you. No more of that. I'll finish it on my own. What could have happened…"

"It wasn't your fault."

And that was so like Helen, to let him off easy.

"I started this," she said, "by going to the police."

"And I'll finish it."

She stared at him. "Finish it and leave town?" He saw the distress in her eyes and he realized then how poorly he'd done at hiding his feelings. They'd gotten too close because he'd started to fall in love with her. Those feelings had compromised her safety, possibly caused him to forget the well-being of his own family. He could not, would not allow that to happen again.

"I've got to make some arrangements," Sergio said, after a deep breath. "I need to move the girls."

Helen flinched. "But..." Then she stopped. "I understand. There was a shooting here and you can't risk whoever was working with Burnette coming back."

"It's probably overkill." He flashed a tired smile. "But since I can't convince you to leave the lodge until it's sorted out, at least I'll know they're safe. It's only for a little while longer. It's my job." He paused. "They're my number-one priority."

She looked closely at him. "Yes, of course. That's what Fiona would want."

It occurred to him just then that Fiona would want her girls to know a woman like Helen, to have her as a mentor, a guide. A mother? Was it a betrayal of his sister even to imagine allowing another mother figure into their lives? He would not think of that, not right now. He cleared his throat. "I'd better go."

"I would love to arrange a birthday party for the girls here. I mean, after everything is calmed down." Her face crumpled. "But I guess maybe that's not something you'd want, away from their friends and everything."

"I'm afraid I haven't let them make too many friends. It's awkward, as a single father, arranging playdates and park outings when most of their peers have their moms handle all that."

"Well Mitch's son Charlie would love to get to know them, and Evonne our desk clerk has a four-year-old daughter who comes often to play. They could all come for birthday horse riding and cake." She was warming to the idea. "And Liam made a piñata for Charlie's birthday. I know he'd..." She trailed off as she caught the look on his face and he could have kicked himself.

"I'm sorry. You're really sweet to think of it, but I better learn how to do these things by myself."

She nodded, shoving a section of hair behind her ear. "Right. Sure. I'll stay up for a while and continue to look at the photos. Maybe something will..."

He shook his head, noting Mitch pulling up to the lodge, letting an exuberant Jingles out of the front seat. "It's okay, Helen. That's a dead end. Get some rest."

He opened the lobby door for her, just as Jingles shot like a rocket to her side, tongue in full lick mode. She knelt, flashed that amazing smile and fondled his ears. "I missed you, sweetie."

The dog didn't know how fortunate he was to have the companionship of the most magnificent woman Sergio had ever met.

Knock it off, Serg. You know what you need to do.

No room for thoughts of Helen or birthdays or the electric shower of sparks caused by their kiss.

He waved at Mitch inside the lobby and started back for the cabin to break the news to the girls that they'd be returning to the hotel. The sky was already nearly black, twinkling with the brilliant pinpricks of stars. As he walked, he texted Chad and made arrangements for what he hoped would be the final leg in his journey for justice.

Tonight, I'm going to find out who killed you, Fiona.

In spite of herself, Helen slept deeply, Jingles curled up on the floor nearby. A sound pulled her from sleep and her eyes flew open when Jingles whined for the second time.

She jerked up so fast her head spun. Panic flashed through her. Her attacker had returned, was her first thought, until she noticed Jingles peering out the small window that looked down over the lodge entrance. She crept over and pulled the curtain aside. Across the shadowed lawn she saw the headlights of a vehicle with a familiar rumbling engine. It was the ranch truck Chad always drove. Jingles could recognize that sound even if his ears were stuffed full of cotton balls. His tail lashed in agitated arcs. She watched as the door of the cabin opened and Sergio jogged to the truck, carrying a dark bundle of supplies.

The truck idled for a moment more and drove off the property. Helen didn't hesitate before she pulled on jeans, a sweatshirt and jacket and slid a heavy-duty flashlight into a backpack. On impulse, she swept up the scanned photos and stowed them securely in a ziplock bag and put them in her pack.

"You have to be quiet," she said to Jingles. He yipped and wriggled his hind end at the prospect of a nighttime adventure.

"Shhhhhh," she hissed. She considered locking him in the room but she knew he was liable to start up a wild hullabaloo at being left behind, so she clipped a leash on him and eased open the bedroom door.

"Going somewhere?"

She jumped to find Mitch in the hallway, in socked feet, with his boots clasped in one hand. "I didn't hear you at all."

He grinned. "I'd like to say it's due to my uncanny tracking prowess inherited from my ancestors, but more than likely it's 'cuz Jingles makes more noise than a herd of cattle. I was going for coffee."

She sighed. "Jingles woke me. I saw Chad and Sergio leaving."

He arched a thick brow. "So you decided it'd be a smart thing to follow them all by yourself?"

She ignored the gibe. "Where are they going, Mitch? Tell me."

"You think I know?"

"I *know* you know."

He shrugged. "They didn't want you to be privy because they have this nutty idea you'd follow them."

"Where?" she demanded. When he stayed aggravatingly silent, she tried to get around him. "Never mind. I already know where. Sergio's going to get into those tunnels through the back entrance I showed him. I'm going too."

"Nope," Mitch said.

She lifted her head so she could look him full-on. "Mitch, you are bigger than me, stronger than me and a law enforcement professional, but if you don't let me by, I am going to start screaming at a volume that will bring everyone running from here to Los Angeles."

He lifted a careless shoulder. "Go ahead. Not my lodge. If you wanna wake all your guests, have at it."

"All right," she said slowly. "Then I will attempt to climb around you and you will be required to forcibly manhandle me to prevent me leaving. Are you prepared to do that to your sister?"

He shifted slightly, blinked and huffed out a breath of defeat, eyes on the floor. "No, ma'am, I am not."

She smiled. "All right then. Let's go, shall we?"

He grumbled as they went. "That was playing dirty."

She smiled as she ran down the stairs with Jingles at her heels.

Mitch caught up with her at his truck. “This is a bad idea on many, many levels.”

“I...” She stopped when his phone buzzed.

He listened to the message, his face turning to stone.

“What?” she said in alarm when he disconnected. “What’s wrong?”

He was quiet for a moment. “Burnette is dead.”

She closed her eyes. “He didn’t survive the fall.”

“He didn’t have a chance to.”

Now she was on full alert as she stared at him. “He didn’t die from his injuries?”

“Someone snuck into his room when the cop on duty was taking a call and smothered him with his pillow.”

Shock shuddered through her senses as they climbed into the truck. Murdered. It could not be. It must not be. But if the murderer was desperate enough to silence his accomplice, what would he do to prevent the tunnels from being accessed again?

“Farraday searched the room he’s been holing up in at the dive shop. They found a cloth saturated with brake fluid. Burnette’s the guy who sabotaged Sergio’s SUV.”

“But whoever is paying him is still out there.” She jerked a look at Mitch. “What if the killer knows about the second entrance to the tunnels?”

Mitch didn’t reply, but he pushed the truck faster.

“We have to warn Sergio and Chad.” No answer on Sergio’s phone, so she tried Chad. “They must be underground already or up in the mountains.” Quickly she texted, with no reply.

“Faster, Mitch. We have to hurry.”

TWENTY-TWO

Sergio and Chad had missed the entrance to the tunnels twice before Sergio finally recognized the moonlit stack of rocks his sister had declared had a resemblance to a stallion. Chad stared upward at the pile. "Doesn't look like a stallion to me."

"I don't see it either, but this is the place." He yanked away the curtain of grass. "I can take it from here," he said, climbing through.

Chad squeezed in behind him anyway. "I think Helen likes you for some reason. I don't, of course, but she does, so I'm gonna babysit you for her sake."

Sergio caught the barest tone of humor which he figured meant Chad was joking. Possibly. "You know how to dive?"

He shrugged. "Used to snorkel with my girlfriend."

"She still in the picture?" he said, realizing it was another of his nosy questions.

"No." That one syllable from his quiet companion held a universe of loss, a world of pain.

He scrambled to change the subject. "So you're not into Scuba?"

"Nah, but I can yell for help if you look like you're drowning."

"That's a comfort."

They got on hands and knees and crawled into a corridor which fortunately widened rapidly to standing room. The walls formed a dank passageway that had probably been paved with stones at one time, though now the floor was pockmarked with muddy holes. The water here was only a slow trickle, enough to wet their boots. Sergio lugged the bag of gear along.

Chad didn't hide his skepticism. "What makes you think you're gonna find anything down there?"

"Because Burnette was paid by someone to keep us out, which means there's something down here."

"Like looking for a needle in a haystack."

"Or a black cat in a coal cellar."

Chad laughed. "Liam would like that one."

They continued on until the tunnel began to pitch sharply downward. Sergio stopped and shucked off his jeans, under which he was wearing a pair of swim trunks. Chad handed him the wetsuit.

"Going to use the tanks?"

"Not for the first entry. The space is too tight. If I'm wrong, I'll surface and get them."

"You sure a snorkel is gonna do the job?"

He shrugged. "Would you like to risk wedging your tank on a rock and drowning?"

"Can't say I would."

Sergio slipped a mask and snorkel around his neck. "Me neither."

A noise echoed along the passageway.

Chad cocked his head to listen. "What was that?"

They both froze. Over the sound of the wind moaning through the corridors, they heard something else, the crunch of rock.

They took up cover positions as best they could, Chad behind an outcropping of rock, and Sergio crouched in the shadow of a jumbled pile of stones. Chad had brought a rifle, but he'd locked it in the truck since the passageway was a tight squeeze in some places.

The sound of movement, the flicker of light told him someone was coming, probably more than one person. Perhaps he should have clued in the police after all, but he didn't trust Farraday in the slightest. Breath held, they waited.

A big shadow rippled over the walls and then Mitch showed up, head bent low to avoid braining himself. Sergio's tension started to dissipate until he saw Helen creep in right behind him.

"Mitch?" Sergio said.

Mitch bent to look as Sergio came out of hiding. "Why did you let her come?" Sergio demanded.

Mitch gave him a pained look. "She made it clear I'm not her boss."

"I don't need anyone's permission," Helen said. "And we have to tell you something."

They relayed the information about Burnette's death. "So you have to get out of here, Sergio." Helen's expression was hard to read in the flashlight glare, but her tone could not be misunderstood. "Whoever killed Burnette is eliminating the loose ends. This isn't safe."

"I agree," he said. "You should leave right now."

"And you too," she tossed back.

He looked to Chad and Mitch for support. "This is our only chance, the last lead we have. I have to go in. Take her home. Please."

"You can't go down there," Helen snapped. "There's no guarantee you'll find anything anyway. Let it go."

Could he? Let the last chance to nail Fiona's killer slip away? Helen's demeanor was stark, pained. Was it possible to hand over vengeance to the Lord? He could, he realized, if it meant that Helen would be safe. He knew in that moment, he would give up everything including his craving for justice, even his life, if it meant saving hers. If that wasn't love, he realized, nothing was. The thought washed over him with the force of a wind-tossed wave. But now it didn't matter; the stakes had gotten too high. He had no other choice.

"Helen," he said. "I can't."

"Yes…" she started.

"The killer isn't going to stop, even if we do. Too many people know we believe there's evidence in these tunnels, Gavin, Justin, Farraday, Allyson. One of them is a killer and they are not going to stop when there's the chance you'll recognize a clue in the photos or find another way down into these tunnels."

"You don't have to do this to keep me safe," she pleaded. "My brothers…"

"Would all agree with me. I have to finish this, or it will never be over for you."

Helen looked helplessly to Mitch and then Chad. "Tell him he's wrong."

Both brothers remained silent until Mitch spoke. "I'll let Jingles out of the truck and take up watch outside."

Chad nodded. "I'll stay here."

He felt cleaved in two when he noticed the tears sliding down Helen's cheeks. He kissed her lightly and whispered in her ear. "It's gonna be okay. Go with Mitch."

"Sergio," she breathed. "The girls…what if…?"

"I'm coming back," he said, "but if I didn't…" He squeezed her tight. "They have an amazing godmother."

She met his eyes then and he saw in her terror, love, resolution and strength that took his breath away. She held his face and pressed a hard kiss to his mouth. "You come back. Promise right now."

He smiled, the golden glow inside him blasting away all the darkness. "Promise." With every scrap of resolve he possessed, he detached himself from her and walked without looking back. Even the frigid water did not overcome the warmth from her touch.

If there was evidence in these tunnels that would set Helen free from the terror, he'd find it.

Somehow, some way, he'd find it.

Helen wanted to pace as she watched Sergio vanish into the dark water, but there simply wasn't room for it in the gloomy space. Chad leaned against a rock, watching the ripples on the surface fade into stillness.

"You love him, don't you?"

Helen jerked toward Chad. "I..." She wanted to lie, to tell him she could not love Sergio because he was Fiona's brother, because he did not want the complication of a woman in his life when he was trying desperately to parent. Instead she wanted to ignore the implication that loving Sergio meant loving his girls, stepping into the role of their mother which he clearly did not want.

"Yes," she said finally. "But it doesn't matter."

"Why?"

"It just doesn't." She wrapped her arms around herself, remembering the batch of photos in her pack. There was no way to help Sergio's underwater mission, but at least she could do her part on the surface.

"Can you bring your light over here?" She hoped the

question would forestall any further comments about what she'd just revealed.

Chad did so, holding it so she could again scan through the pictures. The diner, the funeral, the family photos. What was here in these images that was so significant Burnette had to be killed?

Chad checked his phone. "Liam should be on his way home from the airport just about now. He's gonna be furious when he finds out you're down here."

"Maybe he's mellowed."

Chad snorted. "I don't think the ring on his finger means he's turned into a pussycat."

The ring on his finger... A bolt of energy scorched through her. She flipped back to the first picture, the teens in the diner, the boys holding their burgers, the girls their milkshakes. She took Chad's phone and enlarged the image. Breath caught, she pressed a shaking hand to her mouth. There it was, the innocuous detail that ended the decades of wondering.

"What?" Chad said.

"Look," she whispered, pointing to a spot on the photo. Chad squinted. "The ring? So?"

A shot rang out and Chad catapulted backward, blood seeping from his shoulder as he crumpled to the muddy floor.

Helen screamed, whirling to face the killer.

TWENTY-THREE

Sergio paddled through the watery passage, uncertain if what he'd found was proof of anything. He'd photographed it anyway, put it into a pouch attached to his waist. Bobbing above the water, he was just in time to hear a muffled explosion. Not an explosion, a gunshot. Now he flat-out swam hard, kicking furiously, using his light to shine the way back up until he was in proximity to the place he'd entered. Still cloaked in shadows, he broke the surface as quietly as he could. Two figures stood opposite each other. One was Helen, stiff with tension, talking to a person he did not at first recognize. Chad was on the ground, groaning.

Sergio moved closer, trying to identify the person Helen spoke to, but the man had his back to the water. Sergio opened his mouth to call out when he caught a snatch of Helen's conversation, the fear a live thing in her voice. "How did you get down here past Mitch?"

Justin answered. "There are tons of ways into these tunnels. Burnette told me all of them."

"I need to help my brother," Helen said, moving for Chad.

"He'll be dead right after you so don't bother." He

glanced at the scanned pictures in her hand. "You figured it out finally?"

"At the funeral you told us you'd lost your ring fishing a week before the tunnels," she said. "But it's there on your finger in the diner picture."

Justin Dover laughed. "That's what Fiona figured out, crafty lady. I saw her in a coffee shop going over the photo book and I made the dumb mistake of joining her. She flat-out asked me about the ring, why I'd lied. I made up some story which she didn't believe. I saw her go into the dive shop and I found out she'd rented gear so..." He shrugged. "I had to make sure she didn't make that dive. My ring is still down here somewhere. It was unlikely she'd find it, but I couldn't take the chance she'd recover it or talk about her suspicions. Maybe share what she knew with the cops."

So he'd killed her. Justin Dover had killed Fiona. Rage hummed through his veins, but he had to control it. Helen was moments away from death. Justin moved a hair and Sergio glimpsed the gun. He swallowed down a lump of white-hot anger. *Focus. You'll only get one try at this.* He continued to ease out of the water.

"Fiona was your friend," Helen said.

"Not when she was trying to prove that I killed Trish. It was a lifetime ago. She didn't have to go dredging it all up again. I never did find her photo book after I ran her down. I gave up looking."

"Until I went to the cops with the note Fiona left in the cabin."

"Bingo. When I got wind of that, I searched the place with no success. Worse, I remembered there were three of the rotten albums. Allyson didn't give up hers, because I was watching the day Fiona left her house. She hated her sister anyway, so I figured the photo book was safe with her. So that left yours." He spoke peevishly, as if he was complaining about a game that didn't go his way.

"Why?" Helen's voice cracked. "Why would you kill Trish and let Gavin suffer all those rumors? Let us all suffer?"

"Gavin." Justin spat. "He came out of it fine. The jock, comfortable family, plenty of money. Trish loved him, and he didn't care the slightest bit for her. He deserved to suffer."

"You haven't answered my question," Helen said. "Since you're going to kill me, at least give me the satisfaction of knowing what happened all those years ago."

Sergio's head and shoulders were out of the water. Helen gulped. Had she seen him? *Keep him talking, Helen.*

"I was a dumb kid who liked the wrong girl," Justin said. "I knew Gavin wasn't going to take Trish to prom. He had eyes on someone else. He was just dating Trish to pass the time. I figured I'd ask her before someone else did, so I cornered her in the tunnels. Even took my ring off to give it to her. She not only turned me down, she said she'd never go out with me because she loved Gavin." His chin jutted in anger. "Even after I told her he wasn't going to ask her to prom, she argued. Got mad at me, accused me of lying because I was jealous. I picked up a pipe and hit her with it until she was quiet."

Helen was crying now. Sergio was clear to the waist. Just a few more moments. "Oh, Justin," Helen whispered.

"I flung away the pipe and that's when I realized my ring fell somewhere but I couldn't find it. I rolled her body into the shadows and kept looking as long as

I could." He shook his head. "I didn't mean to kill her. If I had to do it again, I wouldn't. But I'm certainly not going to jail, not after all these years. I was just a kid."

"No," she said. "You were a killer. And you still are. You paid Burnette to go after me and when he was caught, you killed him in the hospital."

He raised a shoulder. "No one will miss him. He got the pipe back for me before he set the explosive and I disposed of it, but he couldn't find the ring, so he was done being helpful anyway."

"So Gavin was completely innocent? What was all that about him renting fishing poles?"

"He's a sheep. I badgered him about going fishing until he rented some poles. I offered to pick them up. Gave me an excuse to go to the dive shop so Kyle and I could talk." He grinned. "You thought Gavin was involved, didn't you? Stick to your day job, Helen. You're no good as a detective."

Sergio moved in the water until he was only a couple of feet from Justin.

"Give me the photos," Justin said, free hand extended.

"Get them yourself." Helen hurled the photos hard at him. As Justin groped to grab them, Sergio hurtled from the water and crashed into Justin with all his strength.

They grappled on the ground. Justin fought fiercely, but Sergio knew he would not be overcome by this man who had taken so much from so many, Trish, her friends and family, Fiona, his girls and Helen. He wrapped an arm around Justin's neck and squeezed.

Justin choked, spluttering for air. Still the rage thundered inside Sergio. Then he felt Helen on her knees next to him.

"Sergio," he heard her say. "Let him go. Lucy and Laurel need you. Please."

Lucy. Laurel. Fiona. Their faces swam in front of his eyes, but the one that eclipsed all others was Helen. He looked at her and his anger melted into something smaller, something that would fit in a spot in his soul until he could fully make peace with it. He released his grip, and Justin flopped forward, gagging. Mitch exploded into the tunnel with another man Sergio didn't know, both with guns at the ready. Liam, Sergio figured. Jingles barked and raced to Chad. Sergio was suddenly so exhausted he could do nothing but sit there as Mitch tied Justin's wrists and Liam sank to his knees to tend to Chad.

"Is he okay?" Helen called, her voice almost a wail.

"He's lost some blood, but he's still kicking," Liam said, his drawl incongruous with his intense military bearing as he drilled Sergio with a look. "Helen, did this clown allow you to be injured in any way?"

She shook her head and sank down next to Sergio. "No, Liam. He saved my life."

And they'd uncovered Fiona and Trish's killer.

Together.

Helen helped him to his feet and they followed Mitch and Liam out of the tunnels, Chad supported between them.

Outside Sergio sucked in a deep breath while Helen held on to his hand. He pulled out his pouch, gingerly easing out an object safely contained in a plastic bag.

The ring glittered in the moonlight.

Tears flooded her eyes. "If he hadn't dropped it, Fiona would be alive."

Sergio let out a breath and something inside him released. "But Trish wouldn't. Fiona set the ball in motion for Justin to be caught. We just finished the job."

She nodded. "You finally have justice."

"We both do," he said, and he knew Fiona would be very pleased with that.

Three days later Helen opened the door to the cabin and hugged Chad, careful not to bump the sling. "How's the arm?"

"Fine. Should be okay to ride, but they won't let me."

"Who?"

Chad jerked a thumb behind him. "Mr. Bossy Pants."

"That'd be me," Liam said, his arm around Maggie. "But Aunt Ginny and Uncle Gus have my back on that one. He's got two more weeks of lazing around like a couch potato, eating bonbons."

Chad grimaced. "I dunno what a bonbon is, but I sure ain't eating one."

Maggie laughed, offering up her pink pastry box along with a squeeze for Helen. "Here's the cake. Decorated with pink-and-yellow roses and little plastic horses, just like you asked. I'll put the ice cream in the freezer."

"Perfect," Helen said. She slid the cake on the table and helped Aunt Ginny adjust the balloons. Out the window she watched Mitch swing Charlie down from his shoulders. The little boy immediately ran off to join Lucy and Laurel and Evonne's daughter as they played with a collection of tiny toy horses she'd purchased especially for the party. Jingles alternated between dogging Liam's every step and racing over to investigate what the chattering kids were up to. Helen had already put a paper birthday hat on the dog, and he'd accepted it with good cheer. Jingles would even tolerate a bath, she figured, if it meant he could be a party guest.

She wanted everything to be perfect, especially since she knew Sergio and the girls would be leaving soon, heading back to southern California. Sergio rolled hot dogs around the grill, enduring good-natured harassment from Liam and plenty of cooking advice from Chad.

Finally, he handed the tongs to Mitch who began to transfer hot dogs from the barbecue to Betty's waiting platter.

Sergio crooked his finger to Helen. She joined him, and they walked away from the barbecue into the dappled sunlight under the oak tree. The children trotted their plastic horses around in the pretend corral she'd sprinkled with straw.

"Good call on the toy horses," he said. "The girls are thrilled. I'm going to make sure I find Fiona's horse collection for them. They're going to love them as much as Fiona did."

Helen smiled. "I'm so glad they are enjoying the party."

"Girls," he called. "Come over here for a minute."

Laurel and Lucy trotted over, still clutching their horses.

"Can you say thank you to Miss Helen for your birthday party?"

"Thank you," the girls trilled.

"You're so very welcome," she said, though it tore at her heart to think that soon the little family would be gone from the property, from her life. But there was nothing here for them, only memories of what they'd lost right in that very town. To cover her unsteady emotions, she bent to cuddle the girls who were hugging her around the knees.

Lucy held up three fingers. “I’m three,” she said, though it sounded like *free*. Laurel nodded soberly in agreement.

Helen smiled. “Yes, that’s right. You’re three now, aren’t you? Your mommy…” she started, then stopped.

“It’s okay to say it,” Sergio said. “We’ve been talking about Fiona today.”

“Your mommy would be very proud of you,” Helen forced out. “She would want you to have a very special day.”

Laurel nodded, still leaning on Helen’s leg. “Daddy said after the cake and balloons, he’s going to do a puppet show.”

She didn’t even try to conceal her amusement. “Daddy is a puppeteer?”

He shrugged. “I’ve been watching YouTube videos. It’s amazing what you can learn that way. I could use some help, though. Can you handle a sock puppet?”

“I’ll give it a try.” She laughed and he linked his arm through hers. She felt tension in him, a ripple of emotion she could not understand. Sadness at their imminent departure? Wistfully, she hoped he would miss her, in some small way that would mirror her own devastation at losing them. It would all be over soon and she’d get back to her life, and he to his. Wounds would heal, or at least they would hurt less over time.

He gestured them all to a bench in the sun, putting his girls on his knees. “Miss Helen was your mommy’s friend, did you know that?”

Laurel bobbed her head. “Mommy loved her.”

Helen swallowed.

“Yes,” Sergio said, looking into Helen’s eyes. “Your

mommy did love her, and you know what? I love her too, very, very much."

Helen sucked in a breath, unsure she had heard correctly.

He went on, bobbing the girls on his knees. "I love her because she tries to do the right thing, all the time, even when people around her don't. She's kind and gentle and she loves God. That's why Mommy loved her, and that's why I love her." He pressed a kiss to each of their temples. "Do you think you could love her too?"

Helen froze, uncertain. "Sergio…"

He nodded reassuringly. "We've talked about it. Girls, what do you think? Could you love Miss Helen too?"

She watched in amazement as both girls nodded and Lucy crawled in her lap and pressed a kiss to her cheek, her feathery hair soft as down. Helen could only hold her lips together to keep the storm of feelings contained.

"All right then," Sergio said. "Laurel, why don't you show your friends where the beanbag-toss game is, okay?"

Laurel and Lucy scampered off, squealing.

"Sergio…" she started again, but he stopped her with a finger to her lips.

"You heard what I have to say. I love you." His brown eyes were soft pools. "It sure wasn't in my plans when I came to Driftwood—I had a big chip on my shoulder about you and what I believed was your fault."

She could not look at him. "It was, partially anyway."

"No," he said. "It was Justin's, and now he's in jail. Case closed." He took her hands. "I want to be with you, to love you and build a life with you and the girls right here in Driftwood."

Though her heart leaped at the words, a shadow of doubt struck at her. "But…would Fiona want me, you know, to be their mother?"

A peace she'd not seen before seemed to have come over Sergio. "Yes, Helen. I've been praying over that a whole lot and you know what? Fiona chose you and I choose you. I am absolutely, one-hundred-percent certain we were meant to be a family." He paused. "So what do you say, Miss Pike?"

Still she could not form an answer.

"It's a lot to tackle, me and two children." He stroked his palm up her arm. He paused, a glint of tears showing. "I know in my heart that Fiona would not want anyone else to be a mother to her girls except her very best friend. I love you and they love you too." And then he stopped talking, looking at her with such tenderness it took her breath away.

Could this be the man God intended for her? Fiona's brother? Could she actually be meant to be mother to Fiona's precious girls? Slowly she felt the burden of the past slipping away, rolling off her shoulders like the mist burning off the seaside cliffs. God did not want her to allow any misgivings or fears to stand between her and the mountain of blessings that He'd bestowed on her. She raised her head then, and fastened her gaze to his, listening to the delighted squeals of the girls who would be hers to love, theirs, knowing he was right, that Fiona would be happy.

"I love you, Sergio," she said. "And I love your girls."

"Our girls," he said, through a glimmer of tears. His smile was wide and brilliant. "How about we get hitched and make it official?"

She laughed through the tears that dampened her face.

"Our girls," she repeated, as he bent close and joined his mouth to hers. "And my answer is yes."

* * * * *

Dear Reader,

As I write this letter it's springtime here in Northern California. The graduation season is upon us. I've been a teacher for most of my adult life, and graduation is such a significant time as our youngsters step out into their next phase. It's a frightening prospect in some ways. There are so many temptations and dangers swirling around this world and consequences for mistakes can be high. Helen experiences just such a thing as she endures the devastation of a youthful dare gone wrong. My own girls have fledged into college students, and I fight the urge to try to keep them tethered close in our safe little family home. What comforts me is the knowledge that the Lord loves them ever so much more than I ever could. What's more, though we are subject to all manner of disasters here on Earth, He has prepared a place for us where troubles will pass away, a perfect world, a "peaceful home." What a comfort, don't you think?

Thank you for reading this third book in the Roughwater Ranch Cowboys series. I hope you will come along with me in book four, which will be youngest brother, Chad's, story. If you'd like to contact me, you can send a message via my website at www.danamentink.com. There's a physical address there also if you prefer.

Thank you, friends, and God bless!
Dana Mentink

COMING NEXT MONTH FROM
Love Inspired Suspense

Available March 3, 2020

FUGITIVE TRAIL
K-9 Mountain Guardians • by Elizabeth Goddard

When an escaped convict vows revenge on Deputy Sierra Young, former coworker turned PI Bryce Elliott is determined to protect her. But can Bryce, Sierra and her search-and-rescue K-9, Samson, track the fugitive before he succeeds in taking their lives?

FALSELY ACCUSED
FBI: Special Crimes Unit • by Shirlee McCoy

Framed for her foster brother's murder, FBI special agent Wren Santino must clear her name—but someone's dead set on stopping her from finding the truth. Now with help from her childhood friend Titus Anderson, unraveling a conspiracy may be the only way to survive.

AMISH COUNTRY MURDER
by Mary Alford

As the sole woman to escape the Dead of Night Killer, Catherine Fisher's the key to catching him—if he doesn't kill her first. But with her memory missing and all clues indicating the serial killer targeted her for very personal reasons, it'll take everything FBI agent Sutter Brenneman has to keep her safe.

MOUNTAIN CAPTIVE
by Sharon Dunn

Private investigator Jude Trainor won't give up on finding a kidnapped little girl—even when the suspect runs him off a mountain road and sends bullets his way. But when Lacey Conrad rescues Jude on her snowmobile, can they outlast a snowstorm *and* a person who wants them dead?

STOLEN SECRETS
by Sherri Shackelford

After she discovers someone's been impersonating her to steal classified technology secrets, Lucy Sutton has to figure out who's behind it. National Security Agency employee Jordan Harris is the only person she trusts. But capturing the culprit is an even deadlier task than they expected.

KILLER HARVEST
by Tanya Stowe

With her boss murdered, Sassa Nilsson's the last person who can save the world's crops from a lethal plant pathogen. But with criminals willing to kill Sassa to get the formula for the virus, can border patrol agent Jared De Luca shield her?

LOOK FOR THESE AND OTHER LOVE INSPIRED BOOKS WHEREVER BOOKS ARE SOLD, INCLUDING MOST BOOKSTORES, SUPERMARKETS, DISCOUNT STORES AND DRUGSTORES.

LISCNM0220

Titus turned onto the paved road that led to town. Wren had said Ryan was there. Ambushed by the men who'd been trying to kill her.

He glanced in his rearview mirror and saw a car coming up fast behind him. No headlights. Just white paint gleaming in the moonlight.

"What's wrong?" Wren asked, shifting to look out the back window. "That's them," she murmured, her voice cold with anger or fear.

"Good. Let's see if we can lead them to the police."

"They'll run us off the road before then."

Probably, but the closer they were to help when it happened, the better off they'd be. He sped around a curve in the road, the white car closing the gap between them. It tapped his bumper, knocking the Jeep sideways.

He straightened, steering the Jeep back onto the road, and tried to accelerate into the next curve as he was rear-ended again.

This time, the force of the impact sent him spinning out of control. The Jeep glanced off a guardrail, bounced back onto the road and then off it, tumbling down into a creek and landing nose down in the soft creek bed.

He didn't have time to think about damage, to ask if Wren was okay or to make another call to 911. He knew the men in the car were going to come for them.

Come for *Wren*.

And he was going to make certain they didn't get her.

LISEXP0220